YELLOW

Dirt

By
R. Allen Chappell

Copyright 2021
R. Allen Chappell
All rights reserved
First Edition
No portion of this book may be reproduced in any form, including electronic or digital media without the express permission of the author or his designated agent.

Dedication

Yellow Dirt, the eleventh book in the Navajo Nation Mystery series, is dedicated to those readers who have so faithfully supported these stories from the beginning. And to those *Diné* who follow the Beauty Way—while their numbers may be fewer each year—they remain the well from which these stories flow. There is no reckoning how many are left who understand the old ways or cling to the ancient traditions, but to them I say, *A-hah-la'nih.*

Acknowledgments

Again, many sincere thanks to those Navajo friends and classmates who still provide "grist for the mill." Their insight into Navajo thought and reservation life helped fuel a lifelong interest in the culture, one I had once only observed from the other side of the fence.

In the back pages, you will find a small glossary of Navajo words and terms used in this story, the spelling of which may vary somewhat, depending on which expert opinion is referenced.

Table of Contents

Tsé Bii' Ndzisgaii	*1*
Independence	*16*
The Campout	*35*
Happy Days	*53*
The Question	*69*
The Suspect	*78*
The Dig	*88*
The Conundrum	*100*
The Folly	*109*
The Escape	*120*
The Calling	*132*
The Consideration	*146*
The Evaluation	*163*
Deception	*178*
The Problem	*186*
The Chance	*196*
Survival	*221*
No Rainbow	*230*
The Anomaly	*242*
The Caldera	*258*
The Problem	*267*
The Calling	*275*
Glossary	*293*

Chapter 1

Tsé Bii' Ndzigaii

"There is little to be said of a person who cannot provide for himself in his own land." A Grandfather's words coming back to haunt the boy in those first hours after his mother's death. This was how the young Sam Klah was berating himself as sunrise brought a blush to the edge of the eastern mesas. Despite the overpowering grandeur of the *Tsé Bii' Ndzigaii*, it can sometimes seem a desolate and barren place, and to those who know the legends, even more frightening.

Hunger gnawed at the boy, though there was little to be done for it. There had been almost nothing to eat in the old *hogan* for days before his mother died...not that there ever was very much. With the sheep gone, there would be even less. The dwelling itself was gradually returning to the earth. Spring rains and summer storms had done their work with a vengeance. With little in the way of resources, the boy and his desperately ill mother found themselves unable to keep up with repairs. The unusually fierce winds and driving rains of summer had made life even more unbearable. The sheep, long sold for lack of feed, left the two with only a pair of old horses as a reminder of how they once had made their living. The horses might have been sold too, but for the boy taking them out each day to graze, secretly knowing he might someday have to go for help.

Despite a long and deteriorating lung condition, death came unexpectedly to the widowed Lyla Klah...as death so often does on the *Dinétah*. Some believed her illness was tied to the scattered plots of yellow earth, and piles of tailings that dotted the area, carelessly left behind by the uranium miners. No one would say this for a fact—only that the woman was not the first to fall victim to the "yellow dirt" as it was called thereabouts. Her husband's death had come when Sam was still a baby, during the early days of the mining boom. A time when men were being lured to the work by offers of desperately needed jobs—the mining company leaving them ignorant of the consequences.

Sam Klah's father was one of the first to succumb to the then unknown malady, leaving his wife Lyla fearing for her infant son's health. The woman immediately abandoned their old place and moved to a distant *hogan* once owned by a relative who had moved even farther away.

The mining company, learning this first wave of deaths was causing others to leave their jobs, some even bringing claims against the owners. The companies quickly went on the offensive. Rumors circulated suggesting the deaths might be due to a witch's curse—one brought by spreading complaints against the mines. Fearing the loss of their jobs, miners and their families were gradually coerced into an uneasy silence. There were a few who questioned...but not one who dared make an outright accusation. The Government, for its part, declared uranium a war time necessity and critical to the defense of the country. They didn't let up and in the end the need for jobs proved stronger than the threat to worker's health. Later, many affected workers came to regret their failure to carry through, feeling they should have stood up for themselves from the start. By then, however, they too had fallen ill and would eventually suffer the inevitable consequences.

As daylight gained a foothold against the black of night, there came the faint grind of a laboring vehicle. The boy lifted his head as the old Ford truck came into view, easing its way down the ridge in the dim glow of its headlights. He watched as the first glimmer of sunrise rimmed the mesa to see the driver navigate his way along the rough track running past the *hogan*. While Sam knew who the truck belonged to, he had seen the person only occasionally these last few years. The man lived some miles away, making him a neighbor in name only, and then only within the context of the vast area. In his current state of mind, the boy had to think a moment to even recall his name.

Only as the pickup truck slowed to a stop near the *hogan* did it finally come to him, *Erwin... Erwin Johnson... that was his name.*

The man had been a frequent visitor after his father's death, often dropping by to see his mother several times a week, bringing a little canned food from the trading post, or occasionally some small shiny thing he thought might take her eye. Eventually Erwin began spending more and more time at their place...often days on end. He paid little attention to Sam, rarely even speaking to the boy. Finally, over the course of a long summer, there came a falling out. The man harangued his mother for several days as they argued over something Sam wasn't old enough to understand. The upshot was that Erwin finally quit coming around and young Sam had nearly forgotten him and his relationship with *Shimá*. Years later, when the subject came up, his mother would refuse to discuss the man at all, saying only that he was a person who wanted too much but gave too little.

"Is everything all right here?" Erwin demanded from a lowered window.

The boy imagined his grim expression made it clear everything was not alright.

Sam could see the man was in a hurry, on his way into town probably, clearly reluctant to involve himself in anything which might delay him.

For his part, Erwin Johnson, didn't feel any particular attachment or responsibility for this boy, but did have the state of his own *Hozo* to consider. Should he disregard so traditional an obligation to help a fellow *Diné* in need? The failing might increase his debt to an already burdened karma.

It was only this last concern that caused Erwin to ask the question again, and this time in an even firmer voice. "Boy, is there something I can do to help you here?" As he waited for an answer, he appeared to be looking the place over, taking stock of the poor state of affairs which somehow seemed to bring a certain satisfaction. A grim little smile flitted across his face but when he spoke again, the man forced a kinder tone. "I'm asking if there is any way I can help you here, boy?" He said this to Sam in old Navajo as most in that country would be inclined to do. It was one of the few places left where a young person might be expected to understand the old way of speaking.

 Sam Klah lifted his eyes to the man with his first thought being that Erwin looked little different than the last time he'd seen him, and that was years ago. He would have thought the man would look some older now, like his mother, but that didn't seem to be the case. Perhaps it was her illness that caused his *Shimá* to look older than she was. For some in that land, the years do seem to pass with little effect, yet there's no denying it's a hard land that favors very few in any regard.

 Slowly, the boy became more aware of a growing urgency in his visitor, a feeling which rankled something deep inside, making the young man uneasy and somewhat leery of the man. Finally, with a helpless sigh he turned toward the *hogan,* and pointed a trembling finger.

 Erwin Johnson could see then that the boy had been crying.

 "*Shimá...*" the boy murmured, and so softly the man could barely make out the words.

As it sank in, Erwin gazed down the road a moment as though lost in a different time, then shaking his head got down from the truck and moved closer to better understand the boy.

"Is Lyla bad sick?" he asked softly but without any visible sign of emotion.

The boy nodded. "She was very sick for a while... but no more." Choking back tears he said. "I came in late from the horses last night thinking she was asleep. This morning I waited and watched to see if she might take a breath or make some movement." His next words appeared to catch in his throat. "There was no life left in her that I could see. After waiting there beside her for a while, I gathered what things I could and came outside." The boy cast fearful glances in the fading gloom. "I was afraid of the *Chindi*," he whispered, then his voice failed and he looked away, unable to continue.

Even in that sparsely settled country, news gets around, and the sad state of the woman's health was common knowledge among the scattered residents of the area. Erwin Johnson, though initially reluctant to become involved, considered himself a proper minded individual who when pressed knew the right thing to do. He stared at the boy a moment or two, then edged over toward the *hogan*, stopping just short of going in, or even peeking inside the shabby little dwelling. Buzzing flies and the faint cloying sweetness of death wafted his way causing him to cover his mouth and draw back. Anyone growing up in those parts knows what death smells like. For Erwin there was no longer any doubt. He straightened and moved away from the *hogan,* as a nearly imperceptible feeling of fulfilment settled over him.

"Well then," he finally managed. "We have some work to do, don't we?" Though he said this with a grim determination, it was clearly all he could manage not to turn and leave the boy alone.

Sam watched as Erwin brought tools from his truck and began giving directions. The two of them fell to tearing wood from a broken corral gate, using it to board up the door of the shabby dwelling. When they had finished, Erwin fetched a small pickaxe. Someone who doesn't know the way of that land might have thought it odd then, to see him knock a hole high in a side of the *hogan*—that the *Chindi* spirit might escape should it take a notion. Some think it takes a while for the evil little phantom to gather itself and most believe it will not fly at all in the dark. This made it reasonable to think it might still be inside, plotting its mischief.

Their boarding up of the *hogan's* door was mainly by way of warning to passersby, letting them know this place now belonged to the other world and posed a certain risk for the unwary. Thus marked, no one would enter, let alone live in this place ever again. It is a custom that has long meant hardship and trouble for those *Diné* who survive the passing of a loved one inside their home. Required by tradition to abandon the dwelling, they are forced to leave and start anew. Even today, in an effort to prevent abandoning the family home, the old and infirm are sometimes, in their last hours, moved outside the *hogan*... assuming, of course, there is time. Once outdoors, the little demon is free to leave if it chooses, that is, should it not prefer to hang around to settle some old score.

When finished with the work, Erwin, as though deep in thought, looked past the boy and in a detached voice, said, "I will let the trader know of your mother's death and what we have done here. He will notify the authorities, and someone will come to take care of the remains." He took great pains not to mention the woman's name for fear this might guide the *Chindi* to them. This is how it has been since the beginning.

With the coming of the white traders, however, much of this burden gradually shifted to them. In the early days a trader might agree to handle the preparation of the remains, and sometimes even interment, relieving reluctant relatives of this onerous duty. Eventually the trader might make himself indispensable to the community. It was smart business to show 'good will' as it was called. It was felt the trader was able to deal with the dead due to the general belief that white men had no soul, and thus were impervious to the *Chindi's* evil threat. To this day, a death may still be handled by a trader in this manner—there in those far reaches of the reservation, where no one is the wiser.

In any case, there was nothing more to be done as far as Erwin Johnson could see. His efforts should make it plain enough to passersby that a dead person's *Chindi* might still be lurking here. He was now satisfied no thinking *Diné* would venture near the place. His duty fulfilled, his conscience now more or less clear, Erwin Johnson thus supposed himself to be free of further obligation.

Now that everything had been done according to custom and to the best of their ability, the man and boy stood uncomfortably staring at one another. Erwin had, in fact, already turned to go when struck by a passing thought. Hesitating only a moment, he determined to say what was on his mind. "I been knowing your mother since we were children. We always were good friends back then. In our later years I left here and we did not see much of one another. But after your father's death from the yellow dirt, we became closer. I told her I was willing to move in here and help with the place, but she refused the offer. She thought it might interfere with some expected settlement from the mining people." He shook his head. "There was no settlement." With an almost melancholy glance at the boy, he gave a heavy sigh and made as though to leave, then turned back for a final word. Believing it only right he should offer some further token of kindness, something that might insure a little more protection from Lyla's *Chindi* should it be bent on retribution for some past misunderstanding. He was thinking, *fixing this thing will only become more difficult if I put it off. It would be best to take care of this now and be done with it, once and for all.*

"Boy I will take you into town; help you find a relative maybe, or at the very least someone of your clan who can help you through this." This small charity, he thought, should be enough to deflect any evil design the malicious little thing in the *hogan* might be conjuring.

The boy nodded his thanks, but was quick to decline the offer, saying in no uncertain terms that he was obliged to remain there. He still had horses to think of, they had to be taken to water, and feed found for them. Then, with a motion of his hand, Sam indicated the brush arbor where an old saddle and a few other poor possessions were piled together in a heap, offering mute evidence this was where he belonged for now. Looking toward the far horizon, he murmured thoughtfully, "I have an Uncle over to the west...and maybe a little north of that, I guess. I will go to see him until I figure out what else to do... I have no other people that I know of."

Erwin Johnson had expected Sam to say this but tried not to look pleased when the boy confirmed it. He thought to himself, *this boy is smart enough to know he would likely wind up at Child Services should he go to town*. Still, knowing it was only good manners and expected of him, he made a last perfunctory attempt...both to ease his own conscience, and to preserve the state of his threatened *Hozo*. Knowing these two things were, in essence, pretty much the same thing.

"Boy, are you sure that's what you want to do? It's a long way to town, and should you later decide you do want to go there, it might not be so easy to find a ride." He was testing the boy and Sam knew it. Erwin frowned and went on. "To go to your Uncle's might be even more difficult. It is a long tough way horseback." He then thought to add one further thought knowing it too, had little chance of being accepted. "There will not be many people in that country who want to help you." This sounded weak and insincere even to him, yet he watched closely to see what effect he might be having on the boy. It quickly became apparent the young man had, as he'd expected, already made up his mind. There would be no changing it.

Sam Klah didn't hesitate in the least. "I'm sure this is what my mother would want. To find my Uncle and go to him—he is my only relative and will be bound to help me. She mentioned this several times herself in the last few days." This was not strictly true, but he wanted to set the man's mind at ease to release him from any further obligation. There was something about this man that urged caution, though he couldn't say what prompted the feeling. "I will be fine. I been to my Uncle's place once before, with my mother, and I still remember the way."

This also was only partially true, he didn't mention the trip had been a number of years back, when he was still quite young...or that he and his mother never actually found her brother's place. They later heard the uncle had moved a good distance from where they thought he lived, but Sam didn't know exactly where that might be. Nor did the boy feel it important to mention that this Uncle was considered a little strange, according to what his mother said over the years. The man had never once, in all this time, made any attempt to visit them or evince even the slightest interest in seeing her, or in meeting his nephew.

Erwin grimly recalled the boy's Uncle from their childhood days when they had often played together as youngsters. Oh, he knew John Etcitty well enough, and he listened now, thinking there were things this boy couldn't possibly know about his Uncle. At this point, he still thought it best not to persist in dissuading the boy. His case had already been made, the expected results now verified. Nodding thoughtfully to himself, the man turned once more to his truck and, giving the boy a curt nod, left him to his own devices. It was not unusual a boy this age should be determined to go his own way. *It could be expected of any Diné boy on the verge of manhood. The journey, hard though it might be, would certainly be more to the boy's liking than surrendering himself to Child Services.* And then too, he thought, *my problem going forward might well resolve itself.*

~~~~~~

As one forged in the crucible of so hard a land, Sam Klah was convinced he would inevitably dredge up the inherent survival instincts to see himself through any adversities that might confront him. This was how the children of the *Diné* are taught to deal with life and had done so through untold centuries. This young man's mind was made up and there was nothing that would change it.

From this time forward Sam Klah would follow his own heart to make what he could of himself. Through the ages man has been driven as much by curiosity as anything else, and it is the young that are more likely to pursue their vision beyond the next mountain, sometimes even farther...should they dream bigger dreams.

Chapter 2

Independence

Sam Klah watched until Erwin's truck was out of sight, and only when the plume of dust had settled itself along the horizon, did he take a deep breath and turn to the old *hogan* wherein lay the last earthly remains of his mother.

"Goodbye *Shimá*," he murmured quietly, with a last forlorn glance, and picked up his halters to begin working his way slowly down to the sage flats to retrieve his horses.

The two old ponies were suspicious of being taken off their picket pins so early in the morning, in the way of their kind thought it might lead to work. Pulling back on their leads, they tossed their heads and stomped their feet in protest. As they grudgingly followed the boy up to the brush arbor.

Pausing at the thought of what he was about to do Sam Klah couldn't help feeling a moment of fear at the difficult and possibly dangerous path he had laid out for himself. From this day forth he must try not to think of his mother—this was the way of his people, even from those ancient times when they roamed far to the north and well before they ventured into this sparse country they would later come to call the *Dinétah*—Navajo land.

It is embedded in the traditional Navajo mind that he should not dwell upon those who are no longer of this world and must be mindful to keep them from his thoughts...never again to mention their name. None of this, however, could stop the tears as the boy saddled the gelding, then packed the mare with those few things he'd saved in the dark of morning. The mare, skittish and wary of the burlap bags slung, from each side of the horn. They clanked and rattled each time she moved, and though she was old, she danced and snorted, stirring the dust which rose in a cloud only to be carried away by an errant gust. A clear and calm day was in the offing. A good day to travel—Sam Klah was at last on his way to a new, and what he hoped to be, a better life.

Thus, with never another glance at the old *hogan*, the boy tore himself from everything he'd known. Taking up the mare's lead-rope he put his heels to the gelding's ribs, sending the reluctant pony upcountry in a ground eating trot, the mare at times hard pressed to keep up. He did not ease up on the old horses until they'd topped the ridge in a lather; only then stopping to let them blow and recover themselves as best their years would allow. Never once had any of the three looked back to their old home.

By noon he judged they had come the proper distance, it was time to veer more to the west, putting the sun to his back as he again willed himself to think no more of the past.

Sam Klah had gained only another mile or two on his new course when he came upon two boys on burros minding a small band of sheep. As he drew closer, he could see from the resemblance between them that they were most likely brothers.

The two spotted him almost immediately and, being curious as young boys are ever wont to be, they kicked up their donkeys, and trotted over to see who he was, and where he was going.

"*Yaa' eh t'eeh,*" the older boy called, pulling hard on the stubborn burro's rope hackamore, reining him in and causing the animal to do that little dance burros do when forced to defy their better judgement.

"Where to...cousin?" The boy couldn't have been more than ten or eleven years old but was obviously in charge of his younger brother, who he now motioned to stay back a ways.

Sam Klah looked the pair over, noting their ragged clothing and worn sneakers, no worse than what he was wearing himself, though these boys did have on new headbands of rolled bandanas. He replied to their greeting in a noncommittal sort of way and watched as the younger of the two edged up even with his brother that he, too, might be a party to the conversation. He seemed the more gregarious of the two despite being a couple of years younger and was clearly determined to have a part in any sort of talk his brother might instigate. It was obvious the pair saw few people out here and probably still fewer strangers. Always, youngsters out here were hungry for news of the outside world and anxious to interact with their peers from far off.

"*Yaa' eh t'eeh,*" the younger boy finally managed but in a thinner less confident voice. "Where to?" he asked mimicking the other. The older boy gave his brother...if indeed that's who he was...a sour look and again motioned him back.

Sam, unsmiling, gave a push of his chin to indicate he was headed west, though the boys had seen this plain enough already. "I am going to see my Uncle." He told them finally, thinking they might by chance know something of the man. "He lives over that way," he said, motioning to the western horizon with a toss of his hand but went no further than that.

"What is your Uncle's name?" the younger boy piped up again, as though determined to have some part in the thing.

Sam tilted his head to one side and studied the smaller boy for a long moment without answering. Then turned back to the older of the two and said, "My Uncle's name is John Etcitty." After waiting a moment, he asked further, "Have you heard of him...maybe you know where he lives?"

At hearing the uncle's name, the two boys exchanged a wide-eyed glance, and the younger backed his burro up a step as though suddenly through talking and thinking now of home.

Sam sensed these boys knew something but asking directly would most likely make them even more suspicious. It was possible, however, they might eventually come back around to it, should he skirt the issue and talk of other things. People out here, he thought, often don't warm up to strangers until they know something about them.

Sam eyed the older boy's burro. "That is a nice little *télii* you are riding, did you catch him yourself?"

The boy smiled a little at this. "No, my father caught this burro for me, but I'm the one who broke him to ride...and my brother's too. There's a lot of wild burros in this place, a person on a good horse can catch one pretty easy...if he knows anything at all about burros."

"Well, I guess your father knows something about them, to catch two as good as those."

The boy beamed. "Oh, my father knows a lot about burros. He's caught a good many. He used to take them to the sale barn at Cortez to sell, but nowadays he says they don't bring enough money to make it worth his time." The smaller boy, intent on following the conversation, seemed determined not to miss a word. He nodded vigorously and for a moment seemed about to say something, regardless of what his older brother might say, but then, thinking better of the notion, he looked down and remained silent.

The older boy, taking a sudden interest in Sam's horses, said in an off-hand manner, as though it was hardly worth mentioning, "That horse of yours is probably too old to catch a burro. My dad says they can run a lot faster than you think."

Sam nodded affably enough, though he thought this insult to his horse to be rude even from so young a boy as this one. "I suspect that's about right." He said, "This old horse of mine probably *couldn't* catch a burro anymore, at least not one as fast as yours, I guess." He was grinning when he said this, knowing this old horse had won a lot of races for his father, when he was younger and suspected he was still fast enough to catch the average donkey.

"So, you say your uncle lives over to the west of here?" The older brother said this with an odd look on his face.

"He did at one time. I'm not so sure now." Sam let it lie, hoping the boy might pick up the thread of the conversation and let slip something that might prove helpful. He was near certain now that these boys knew more than they were letting on.

The younger of the two could no longer contain himself and raised his voice with a concerned look. "Does your uncle have one eye? If he does...they call him Johnny One Eye around here...if that is him. They say he knows magic!" And here he paused at the enormity of what he was about to say. "It is said he is a witch, and that he will sometimes eat little children, if he gets a chance!"

His older brother threw the boy a sharp glance and turning to Sam declared, "My brother doesn't know what he's talking about. We don't know nothing about your Uncle." He then whirled around to the smaller boy and slapping his burro on the rear caused him to jump and take off in a fast trot. The older brother falling in behind the younger, continued popping the animal with the end of his *mecate*, staying close behind him until they were well across the shadowed valley floor and once again among their scattered flock. Even at that distance Sam could see the pair was turned toward him and watching to see which way he would go.

~~~~~~

By late afternoon Sam was urging the jaded old ponies across yet another rocky rise, but this time was surprised to see the welcoming sight of a good swale of grass on the other side. While rare enough in itself, this particular grassy basin showed a patch of darker green at its head. Thinking this might offer promise of water of some sort, a spring or maybe a small catch-basin where run-off had pooled. He pulled the horses to a stop, pausing a moment to study the little basin. As he watched, he considered the possibilities. Moistening his lips with the last stale drops from his canteen, he fervently hoped there was some sort of water at the head of this valley. It might be a very long time before they ran into any kind of water again.

As he sat his gelding, squandering another minute or two scouting the surrounding countryside, he spotted the almost indiscernible form of a *hogan* on the far side of the little valley. It blended so perfectly with the adobe hill behind it he almost missed seeing it and then couldn't help taking a further moment to wonder who might live in so isolated a place. A simple mud-plastered cedar log dwelling, much like the one he'd called home until this very morning. This one, however, looked recently built yet purposely situated to avoid detection. With no sign of livestock corrals, garden or other usual means of support, he couldn't imagine how these people got along. Seeing the camp brought an unbidden thought of his old home and that one who was now gone and not to be thought of again.

 Finally, forcing his mind back to the business at hand, he made a closer study of the dwelling. There was absolutely no sign of life or recent activity. No smoke from the stove pipe or bedding hung to dry on the bushes. Possibly these people were gone to town...or maybe visiting a neighbor, hard as that might be to believe. He hadn't crossed a road or seen any sign of another camp the entire day. There were no out-buildings, fences, or even corrals of any kind, and he wondered again who had lived here and to what purpose.

 Nudging his gelding, he finally turned the pony toward the upper end of the valley, and its promise of water. Picking his way carefully along the faint and rocky game trail which ran toward the upper end of the valley he kept an eye out for sign of anyone who might recently have come this way. About half-way there, he did come across a few burro tracks heading in his direction *wild burros most likely— perhaps on their way to water.* This encouraging sign brightened his hopes considerably and caused him to hurry his animals along.

Coming to the head of the basin, he saw two long ears above the sage, and then the cautious eye and nose of a jenny burro, followed by two smaller heads peering around her. All three were dark grey with a black cross on their withers, his favorite color when it came to burros. He pulled up and watched them for a moment as they in turn, looked him over. He was still far enough off to prevent them from becoming unduly alarmed. The trio had been lazing in the shade, possibly after drinking their fill, and loath to leave the shade of the little copes of juniper. In this, the hottest part of the day, the burros would likely stay put, should these newcomers keep their distance. The mother and two youngsters, about a year apart from the looks of them, studied him with their great ears perked forward, curious yet alert for the slightest sign of aggression.

When finally, he urged his horses a little farther along the trail, the jenny snorted and threw up her head causing all three to whirl and break into a trot for higher ground. They were fat and in good condition for the time of year. Sam had always liked burros and watched this little family go with a smile on his face. Burros are smart and they are tough, just the attributes required to survive in this sort of country. They had few natural predators to speak of, save the occasional cougar who might decide to take one on. Even then, an adult burro could often hold its own. Quick and deadly kickers, even the more ambitious old dog coyotes gave these small equines a wide berth.

The water, as it turned out, proved to be a tiny spring issuing high in a clump of mountain mahoganies before falling into a manmade catch-basin of smooth laid stone; there were possibly as much as fifty or sixty gallons of sweet water there, a lot in that country considering how dry the season had been. The *hogan* he'd spotted lay a good distance from this water, and he figured he wouldn't be encroaching should he stop to fill his canteen and let his horses drink.

As an unwritten rule of the land, unfenced water on the vast open range of the *Dinetah* is thought to be a public resource and to be shared according to need. Still, he would have asked permission should anyone been about...it was only good manners. His mother had trained him from an early age to follow the more traditional way of thinking.

Someone had stuck a piece of pipe into the substrate at some time or other and it ran a small but steady stream of clear water. He dismounted and proceeded to top up his water bottle, then filled his belly right from the pipe thinking this might fend off his nagging hunger. The water was cool, and his horses were already drinking their fill from the little stone tank.

From this higher vantage, he again took a hard look at the *hogan* he'd seen on the other side. Even from this angle, he could see no sign of the dwelling being occupied...nor could he find any real reason to think it abandoned.

Leading the horses down the steep and rocky trail from the spring, he made his way to the far side of the basin. In all his travel that morning he had not seen a single other human habitation and it occurred to him this place might be such that no one was able to scratch out an existence here and decided to move on. He could see now there was not enough grass to graze the number of sheep or goats required to make a living... not for very long anyway. Even just a few cows would have soon depleted the available resources. Then too, he thought as the brunt of summer came to bear, the little spring that allowed such initial hope, might dry up completely, leaving what feed there was to disappear.

On a happier note, the boy did see a good bit of rabbit sign among the tall grasses, causing the pain in his belly to return with a vengeance, and he thought of the slingshot stuck in the back of his belt. These rabbits would be cottontails and easier prey than their larger cousins. What few jackrabbits were left, would be down on the open flats and much harder to take with a slingshot. He knew he could set a few snares for these smaller *Gah'*, but then he would have to wait until evening for the shy creatures to begin moving about to be caught in his trap. There would be little hope of filling a snare before the next morning. No, the slingshot would be best for now.

The overflow from the catch-basin wended its way down a little gravel strewn bed that reached almost to the *hogan* itself, where it was then caught in a smaller rock basin, much smaller than the upper catchment and holding no more than a few gallons. Still, Sam reckoned, this was more than enough for one or two person's needs. There was no sign of a road into the place, not even an old wagon track. *Whoever lived here came and went horseback* was his final guess and he wondered at such a thing in this day and age. Inspecting the place further he could see no trace of anyone having lived here...not recently. A few dead cedars up the ridge had been cut for firewood in the past, but not for some time.

He unsaddled his horses and made camp uphill, on a grassy bench away from the *hogan*. It was plain someone had camped here in the past. Unrolling his blankets close to a small rock fire-pit, he prepared to spend the fast-approaching night. After staking out the mare to graze, he turned the gelding loose (knowing full well the horse wouldn't leave the mare). Taking the slingshot from his back pocket, he unrolled the long leather thongs attached to the heavy cowhide patch. Picking up a few small smooth stones that were lying about he put them in a front pocket as he moved away from camp to find a rabbit. It was beginning to cloud up and *Gah'* would soon feel safe venturing out.

The boy was back in camp after only an hour, a skinned cottontail at his belt and a green stick to use as a spit in hand. Gathering dry cedar kindling from the remains of a down tree, he soon had a bed of coals to prop his dinner over. Sitting well back from the smoke and embers he relaxed on one elbow and sipped at his water bottle till the rabbit on the spit was done to his liking.

He had never been on his own like this and found the essence of these small freedoms exhilarating. With a full belly, the future of his journey seemed less daunting, less than it had only that morning. As day faded to dusk and darkness fell over the little basin, the various stars he'd come to know since a young child began to appear. He smiled to himself that these old familiar heavens were there to keep him centered on his journey. The star at the end of the "Little Bear" was the compass that led him, and he marked on the ground each night which way he was to head the next morning.

Once more the words of his Grandfather came wafting back on the evening breeze. *There is little to be said for a person who cannot provide for himself in his own land.* The old man would be happy to see his Grandson was a person able to fend for himself and not be lost in a land which was known for being difficult to find one's way.

The next morning, as the glow of dawn edged its way over a far eastern rim, the boy woke not knowing where he was for a moment. He'd slept soundly through the night, with no bad dreams, and this alone made him think things were looking up. This would not have been the case should the *Chindi* have followed him. He felt rested and looked forward to what the day might bring. There still was a haunch of grilled rabbit placed high in the crotch of a juniper tree, and though a bit dry, he was, nonetheless, happy to have it, chewing as he went to the edge of the camp and looked down to the *hogan,* trying again to feature in his mind the people who had built it.

After checking his horses, and finding them still a little drawn, he took them to drink at the little rock-lined depression beyond the dwelling. Even after drinking their fill and resting several hours they still appeared gaunt and tired. This was the way with old horses— unable to recover from a hard ride as easily as they once had. After thinking it over, he decided to stay another night, that his ponies might gather themselves. He took them back to their tethers, and pulled the picket pins, moving the ropes to fresh grass. They hadn't cleaned up the old grass as well as they might have but the boy thought the advantage of fresh pasture might entice them to eat more. They might not be so lucky at the next camp.

During the day he set a few snares, not far from camp and easy to check, then fell asleep on his blankets in the shade of a cedar. Later, coming awake to the neighing of a horse, he knew his ponies had their fill of the good grass and were thirsty and wanting water. After taking them to the little basin, he put them back on their tethers and then fell back asleep for a short while. Refreshed, the boy spent the afternoon sorting and repairing his scant supply of gear. When he was satisfied he'd done what he could to ensure these things were as serviceable as he could make them, he went to check his snares.

Finding two fat cottontails was a welcome surprise. He quickly dressed them and brought them back to hang in a tree to cool before his next meal. Most people will eventually tire of eating rabbits grilled over a fire, but the boy thought himself fortunate to have this bounty so near at hand and enjoyed the freedom from hunger this afforded. He had not had the luxury of such easy meals in their old place.

As the sun fell lower in the west and dusk came on the wings of a cool breeze, he couldn't keep his mind off the *hogan,* drawn to see if he couldn't discover what its story was.

Making his way down the hill to see what he could find that might provide some clue as to who owned the mysterious dwelling, determined now to discover who lived there.

A thin drift of sand lay against the east facing door. His thought was that no one had come or gone for some time. Surprisingly enough, the door appeared to be neither locked nor barred, as one might anticipate.

Taking a deep breath, he reached for the handle and despite feeling he was about to do something which could have unknown consequences, the boy tugged a little until, with a loud creak the pine slab door opened a crack—but only far enough to peep in. Little could be seen in the fading light. Across the top of the *hogan,* the last glimmer of sun from the west shone directly in his eyes.

Though the boy was of average height, he had to stoop a little to peer inside the low doorway for a closer look. Still, he was unable to see beyond a scattering of dust speckled shafts of dim light entering from around the upper end of the stove pipe. A draft of damp, fetid air wafted from the darkness with an almost physical presence. A chill had unaccountably crept over him, along with a near certain premonition that some hidden thing was watching. Waiting, as though deciding how near to let him come. Of a sudden, the boy felt weak and so frightened he was unable to make himself take the thing any further.

Sam shivered in the warm air, quickly pushing the door shut, before he could change his mind. He backed away from the dwelling with a singular thought in mind: *What if someone died in this place and no one found them? What if the Chindi has been here all this time waiting for someone to come along and release it?*

Having come from so recent a death camp made the danger even more real. Now totally unnerved, the boy backed further away. So firmly was he caught in the grip of this imagined horror, he failed to hear the silent threat from behind. Then there was only a sense of falling, drifting downward into a black hole of nothingness, and a vague, dreamlike impression that someone was calling his name.

Chapter 3

The Campout

Tribal Investigator Charlie Yazzie sweated in the noonday sun, his shirt already damp. Prying out a rock the size of a basketball in this flinty ground was proving to be hard work. He couldn't help wondering if his increasingly desk-bound lifestyle had anything to do with this lack of endurance. He doubted it. There had been plenty of work at home to keep him in shape. Still, since his last promotion he had been tied more and more to the office with less and less time in the field.

This particular rock, larger than he'd first judged it, proved to be a small boulder really, but having decided this was the best place left to pitch their tent—the rock being in the way meant it had to come out. Once set in motion, Charlie was not apt to abandon a plan due to its difficulty. Good places to pitch a tent were at a premium along this creek, and this spot would allow them to feel the morning sun on the canvas. Being well toward the end of summer, the nights were cool until the sun was well above the canyon rim. As he rose from his task to groan and stretch his aching back, he couldn't help smiling over at Harley Ponyboy's camp. The little man was still busy trying to lay out his tent, but the help of the irrepressible Harley Jr. was proving more of a chore than he'd anticipated. The boy's father had already turned down help from several other of his fellow campers, saying tersely, "I've almost got it," though it was plain to see he'd barely begun. Earlier he'd tied a rope around his young son's middle, attaching it to a small sapling, which he felt would tether the boy out of the way and provide him a little shade at the same time. As a child, he had been tethered the same way himself and even now felt no harm had come from it.

Finding himself fettered beyond his tolerance, the strong willed three-year old clouded up and threw such a screeching fit he had to immediately be turned loose—then watched like a hawk as the work progressed. The creek meandering through the makeshift campground, proved to be a magnet for the child...as it would for any small boy. The little rebel insisted on splashing about in the shallow water, causing even more consternation among his fellow campers.

Sue Yazzie, tiring of all the noise and commotion, sent her son and daughter to watch the three-year-old until someone could help his father set camp. Joseph Wiley, and his younger sister Sasha, were two of the few people little Harley would pay the slightest attention to, and then for only a short length of time. The little boy was taking his "terrible twos" well beyond that predicted age. Sue, not taking her eyes off the children for a second, shook out her long hair and began rewrapping it in a bun on the back of her head before pitching in to help Charlie.

The Begay camp, with the help of their teenage daughter, Ida Marie, was already neatly set up and on the best spot on the creek too. Coming in at the front of the caravan that morning, Thomas had made certain of that. He had never been a fan of this camping idea to begin with, and groused, "We're Indians for God's sake! We basically been campin' out our whole life, and now that we took the trouble to build ourselves a real house—everyone suddenly decides it's a good idea to get back to nature." He looked around with a cheerless smile of satisfaction, saying to himself, "At least we'll be off to ourselves here and on a nice soft flat spot, away from the noise and dust everyone's stirring up."

Thomas's wife, Lucy Tallwoman, was still busy bringing in bedding and arranging things to suit her idea of how camping should be. She stopped to gaze at her husband a moment and said with a frown. "It's only for a week Thomas. It will be good for the kids. They need to experience this sort of thing. It's part of their culture, you know." Now a Tribal Councilwoman, Lucy had grown used to speaking her mind...and being listened to...even by Thomas, who did not often listen to anyone.

Her husband snorted and grinned over at their friend Harley's camp. "Culture? We'll see what little Iron-Pants Ponyboy over there thinks of his culture when it's time for his cartoons to come on and he can't locate a television set." Thomas grinned maliciously at the thought. "I bet you'll all see a real war-dance then. That's culture."

Lucy threw up her hands in a huff and saying not a word in return went to bring the food coolers from the truck.

The women had been planning a camping trip for months and, when finally, the children had a long school holiday and everyone's schedule seemed to come together at the same time, Sue Yazzie declared it was now or never. Her friend, Lucy Tallwoman, heartily agreed. The two had been close a long time and were generally of a like mind when it came to these things. They left camp for the parked trucks laughing at little Harley's antics, then began unloading the coolers as they talked.

"Why did Harley bring three mules along, little Harley can't ride a mule by himself yet?" Even after all these years, Lucy was sometimes perplexed at how Harley Ponyboy operated, especially now that he had a little money. Everyone thought the money would be gone by now, but the man continued to confound them by intimating he had actually been increasing his worth through various investments, though he wouldn't say much beyond that.

Sue reflected on this a moment. "I was wondering about those extra mules myself." Then said, "Thomas and Charlie brought two horses each so there would be enough for the kids to ride if they wanted." Sue had been a little suspicious why they needed horses at all, though later admitted this seemed a beautiful and interesting piece of country to explore. And Charlie *had* mentioned there was a lot of history in the area.

"Well, I'm out here to get away and relax for a while. They can do what they want with those horses." Lucy had been a good rider when she was younger but now didn't have time to ride as she once had. "Horses seem like a lot of trouble for what little use these guys will likely get out of them."

Sue nodded thoughtfully and smiled, "Whose idea was this place, anyway? For a family campout it seems a long way off the beaten path. I didn't realize how far these guys were talking about going... It must be some macho thing."

Lucy was looking back the way they'd driven in that morning, canting her head slightly in surprise. "Uh-oh, looks to me like we have company. I thought the boys said we'd have this place all to ourselves." She pointed up the creek at a pickup truck with a two-horse trailer behind it. The two women watched as the vehicle came picking its way through the cottonwoods scattered along the little stream.

Sue shaded her eyes with one hand. "Uh... that looks like George Custer's truck and trailer to me." Charlie didn't say anything about inviting the Professor along. "Not that I mind," she quickly admitted, "Everyone likes George... He's a whole different person since he quit drinking...almost like part of the family now. Charlie thinks the world of man and sticks to his every word, but that's not always a bad thing either."

Looking back up the trail, Lucy concurred with a quick nod and said, "Well, we'll know in a minute, here comes Charlie with Thomas, and they're grinning like they know something we don't." The older woman then shook her head and with a half-smile added. "Those two are up to something. I'd bet on it. This is all starting to make a little more sense."

"I wouldn't doubt it a bit." Sue flipped a lock of hair out of her eyes and studied the truck. "Looks like we're going to have quite a crowd up here. I hope we brought enough food, it's a darn long way to town."

Lucy nodded agreement. "I'm just glad my father decided to stay home with his grandson who, you might have heard, has a girlfriend now. I expect that's why Caleb agreed to stay home with Paul in the first place. Paul does well enough on his own these days, but someone needs to be around to talk him out of any silly notions. He still says the sheep need to be taken to fresh pasture every day. They don't, really, but that's what he's putting out. He just likes going out with 'em, but we still think he needs someone along...just in case. We still have hay put back, and he could just as well dry-lot them till we got back, but you know my dad. He insists we not waste hay when there's plenty of grass right there above the house; he keeps saying the 'He Rains' will be along any time now and then we'll be fine without the hay."

Sue smiled thinking of "Old Man" Paul T'Sosi. "I was wondering why your son didn't come along—so, Caleb's got a girlfriend now, has he?"

"Oh yeah, and a cute one, too. She's a friend, from school, Imogene Nez. He's known her since they were in grade school, but apparently it's just been lately that he realized she's a girl...so, you know, everything's different now." She chuckled, "Her family has a little money, I guess, she has her own car, which is good because it will be a while yet before Caleb gets one. Thomas said he would give him his old diesel truck...but that didn't stir up much interest on Caleb's part." Both women laughed at this, nodding at one another as though it was part of some secret joke no one else seemed to get.

Sue sighed. "Thank God, Joseph Wiley hasn't discovered girls yet, it's all we can do to keep him at home now. What with basketball practice and track three times a week it's hard to stay up with him."

The women's husbands also spotted the new arrival and were smiling as they straggled up, ostensibly to help carry the coolers. Thomas stepped up and immediately took charge of explaining George Custer's arrival, hopefully before the barrage of questions might make a mountain he couldn't climb. Charlie let him take the lead, the man was a fast talker when need be, and didn't mind bending the truth. He likely could handle this better than him.

"Ah, I see Doc Custer has finally made it back from town." Thomas said this as though it was common knowledge George would be coming in.

Lucy again looked up the creek and frowned to see the truck hardly slow down as it hit the water with a lurch and a splash. "He's coming in a little hot, isn't he?"

Thomas smiled and nodded. "That's the Doc's style, he likes to make a big entrance. He's probably in a hurry to get back to the 'dig'. He doesn't like being away when he's got a project going on... always in a rush to get back. That's the Doc."

"Dig? What dig? What are you guys up to, anyway?" Lucy eyed her husband, and then turned to Sue's husband, "Okay, Charlie what did you two rope us into now? I thought this was supposed to be a relaxing little family vacation?"

Sue Yazzie stood beside her friend with arms folded across her chest and a grim set to her jaw. She knew her husband had a hard time refusing his old Professor a favor, even at the expense of previous plans. "Charlie, you didn't bring us up here to help out on some archeological site... did you?"

Lucy was quick to jump in. "George Custer didn't talk you boys into helping out up here, did he?"

"That's not it at all, Sue. When George heard we were planning a little campout he just mentioned he was working a site in a beautiful spot for camping and invited us to join him for a few days. It's just him up here by himself and he's got his hands full. He went back into town last night for his trailer. He has a collection of specimens to take back to Farmington. Apparently, he's a little late getting back, that's all."

Thomas chimed in, "That's right Sue, we really didn't expect to see much of him up here, he's working a good way back in the canyon from what he told us." Thomas said all this with a straight face and no trace of a smile.

Sue only nodded, muttering, "Uh huh." before turning back to her husband. "Just how long has George been up here?"

Charlie wasn't good at lying and he knew it. "About two weeks, I guess. He told us it had taken him a lot of that time just to pack in his camp. He hand-carried everything up there and would have to pack out all the specimens the same way. He's already behind in his contract obligation, Sue. He thinks he might lose this client if he doesn't come through on time." He watched George pull into the clearing. "He's not as young as he used to be, and this dig has been hard on him. To tell the truth I'm a little worried about him."

Given the opening, Thomas was quick to step in with a more forthright stance. "The Doc has been good to us, you all know that. He gave Harley and me work when we really needed it, even when he couldn't afford it, and he saw that we got paid on time, even when *he* came up short on his own end. A person can't just blow off something like that. To be honest, we owe the man, this is little enough payback for all he's done for us over the years."

Charlie nodded agreement. "Sue, we can't just stand by and watch him lose everything. It's not going to take much of our time. We'll have things squared away before you know it and still have plenty of time to enjoy our vacation."

Lucy Tallwoman seemed thoughtful when she answered. "Well, I guess it will give the kids a chance to pick up some of that culture I've been talking about. I doubt there's anyone better than George to explain some of this stuff to them. They should know about the history of this area and all its people—many of them were here long before us." She struck a thoughtful pose. You know the Tribal Council has been discussing this very thing lately and the upshot is, here on the reservation the Navajo Nation is responsible for many of these ancient sites, and more needs to be done to educate people who live out here in the back country." She looked down at the ground for a moment with a shake of her head. "I suppose this is as good a time as any for our children to learn to appreciate those who came before us."

Before Lucy had even finished talking to her friend Sue was already nodding along with her, looking off toward the Professor's canyon as though she'd like to see what was up there for herself.

Both men were surprised by this little talk of Lucy's—neither one was aware the Council was taking such an interest in the preservation of past cultures.

Professor Custer was already out of his truck and headed their way. With a smile he greeted each one individually as was to be expected. Then he addressed the group as a whole. "Looks like you folks have been busy. Sorry I was gone when you got in...I should have been here to help you set up. Maybe in the morning we can take a hike up to the site and I'll explain what's going on up there. I think the kids might enjoy that." And as an afterthought, "This is about as far as we can go by vehicle." He looked past them at the camp, then turned to Thomas. "Looks like one of you set your tent right over those burials I found last month. I tried to level things off when I was through confirming the nature of the interments—probably why someone thought it would make a nice flat place to pitch their tent." He waved the thing away, "I wouldn't worry about it, it won't bother them if it doesn't bother you."

Lucy Tallwoman turned to Thomas and gave him a look. "Nice flat place to set the tent, huh? Best spot on the creek, huh? Looks like you need to get busy clearing some brush, while I start moving our things!"

Charlie grinned at his old friend and whispered privately, "If it were me, I'd just stay right there where you are," then turned away laughing, knowing that wouldn't be happening.

After stopping to think about it, Thomas couldn't help grinning himself. Then he pointed up to the camp, slapped Charlie on the back, and smiled. "I don't suppose you'd mind helping us move camp now, would you wise guy?"

Sue Yazzie frowned at the two men. "You two are a 'Mess'...you know that? You're both just a mess!" Then turning back to her friend, she gritted her teeth, "Come on Lucy, I'll help you get your stuff out of there."

It was about that time that Harley Ponyboy came up the trail, dragging Little Harley by the hand. He waved at George while ignoring his son who was squalling and holding out his arms to be picked up. "Up, dada up!" The boy was dripping wet from top to bottom.

Sue now turned her ire on the boy's father. "Why don't you pick that baby up, we could use a little peace and quiet around here."

"I would pick him up, Sue," Harley pointed at the boy's pants, "But not all of that is creek water...that's why I don't. It's warm enough out—this'll all dry in a little while—I just don't want it drying on my clothes."

Sue gave him a cross look and declared. "Well, La de dah, haven't we gotten particular?"

Harley looked down at the boy and then, at his fancy western shirt. It was his favorite, and he'd been taking care not to get it dirty. He nodded his head. "He'll dry," he said it again finally, and this time more firmly, He then went up to Doctor Custer to shake his hand. Little Harley who happened to like the Professor, stopped crying immediately and grabbed hold of George's pant leg to give him a hug.

"Don't do that Harley, you're getting George all wet." The boy's father shook a finger at him. "No, no Harley."

The professor reached down, patted the boy's head, then declared with a smile, "That's okay, Harley... it'll dry..."

Thomas, frowning again at the notion of moving his ill-placed camp, and at the array of heavy coolers left to be transported, was thinking, *this is just about how I thought this camping trip was going to go.*

George Custer grunted as he hefted one of the coolers and taking a deep breath headed uphill to the campground. Charlie already holding one of his own coolers fell in beside him.

"George, we've got everything ready to pack a load down from the site in the morning. Harley brought three mules, three or four packsaddles and some fancy box panniers for the more fragile stuff—Thomas and I brought a couple of extra horses if we need them, too."

"Well, I appreciate that, Charlie, it's been damn good of you boys to offer your help like this." George, now trying to catch his breath, had to hesitate a moment before going on. "You may as well know... There may be something headed this way you're not aware of."

Charlie Yazzie half-turned, and with a surprised look on his face, asked, "And what would that be George?"

"On the way out of town this morning, I stopped to fill up the truck and Billy Red Clay pulled in across the pumps... He looked to me like he was a little put out and asked if I knew where you people were this morning. He said he'd been trying to get ahold of you or Harley and couldn't get anyone to answer their phones. He'd even tried calling his Uncle Thomas, but said it was the same at his house." The Professor stopped and set the cooler down. "I told him you boys were headed up here to the dig for a week-long camping trip with the families. I asked him if it was anything serious, and should I give you a message to call in, but he said no, he was getting ready to come up to this area himself. He said he'd had a call from a trader up this way about a woman dying and thought he better look into it. He acted like he didn't want to say any more about it—but as I was getting ready to go inside to pay up, he wanted to know exactly where you boys were camped and how to get out here." George stood up straight and took another couple of deep breaths before continuing. "He said he'd try getting you on his radio, but after learning where you were, doubted there was much in the way of radio reception out this way."

Charlie touched his tongue to his upper teeth and thought a moment. "Hmm... well, it's Saturday, so I guess he knew I wouldn't be in the office. I can't imagine what he's got going on. I haven't worked with Tribal on anything for a week or so. Lately it seems I don't get a chance to talk to Billy much. Since he became Liaison Officer to the FBI, he's kept a pretty tight schedule. Billy Red Clay is a good officer and doesn't usually ask for help unless it's something serious."

"He sounded serious to me..." George picked the cooler back up and started off up the trail. He was soon huffing and puffing but Charlie could see he was determined to make it all the way to camp this time. Charlie fell back in behind George and as the trail narrowed, kept an eye on his one-time professor. They'd been right to come he thought. His old friend and mentor seemed just about worn out.

That evening as everyone sat around the fire, the men watched in eager anticipation as the women put together a huge pot of beef stew. Sue and Lucy had started it hours before, when the men were pitching in to move the Begay camp to a spot without burials. The move had entailed considerable work, clearing a new spot, and digging out several large rocks. Still, it was accomplished with an agreeable attitude and much good-natured comradery.

The three younger members of the group, under the watchful eye of Ida Marie Begay, spent the latter part of the afternoon gathering firewood and hauling water from the creek, when they weren't busy chasing each other up and down the little stream. Thomas's daughter, as the eldest of the children took charge of the younger ones, including the rascally little Harley Jr., whose antics occupied fully half the other's time. It was the sort of picture-perfect Autumn day the Four Corners has long been noted for—crisp air and turquoise skies set off by a splash of golden cottonwoods against red canyon walls.

Even Thomas had to admit a sense of nostalgia for a traditional life that was fast disappearing. As a boy his people had often moved camp to follow the sheep and the life was not unlike this.

Charlie was moved to agree. "These children will remember this trip for the rest of their lives—it will become part of what they think of when they consider what it means to be *Diné*."

Harley Ponyboy watched as the youngsters chased one another in the bright Autumn sun. He had come up a lot harder than the others but was pleased his son would have a different view of what it means to grow up Navajo. It brought a smile as he regarded his circle of old friends, realizing how lucky he and his son were to have them.

Chapter 4

Happy Days

George Custer, after having a quick bowl of stew, left late in the afternoon for his dig up-canyon, saying, "I have just enough daylight left to make it up there without stumbling along in the dark. I still have a number of items to catalog and make ready for packing out tomorrow." As the Professor called his goodbyes, he made it clear how appreciative he was of the help his friends had so freely offered. Though everyone had prevailed upon him to stay longer, the man was determined to be on his way and started off among a chorus of good wishes.

After a hearty and well-earned dinner, the group sat around the fire going over the day's happenings, all the while agreeing how enjoyable it had been to step away from their regular routines. Little Harley, along with Sasha Yazzie, sat sleepy eyed and nodding off as they listened to the adults recount each child's contribution to the job of establishing camp. It was not long after, the women decided it time to settle the children in the tents for some much-needed sleep. Harley Jr. again declared his dogged intent to sleep in the tent with Joseph Wiley and Sasha. Having heard this from the little boy all day long, and now too tired to argue, Sue said that would be fine. After signaling Harley Sr. their intent, she pointed at the boy and took him in tow.

Navajo children are traditionally indulged rather than force a confrontation. Though Sue was stricter than most in this regard, she admitted to letting little Harley get by with more than she had with her own children. She knew the baby had been through a rough stretch in his first years and made allowances in his behavior on that basis. Living close by and having him frequently in her care, she had become more or less a surrogate mother for the young Harley Ponyboy. She often vowed she was going to tighten the reins, but so far had not done much with that.

When the women and children were in their beds, the three men stayed sitting around the fire talking quietly among themselves. One noted a few clouds moving in to dim the stars and wondered if the weather people had called for rain this weekend. The other two thought not.

Thomas allowed as how George Custer seemed pretty excited about his work up-canyon. Charlie threw a glance in his direction as he shook his head. "I don't know, I think the Doc had mixed emotions about taking this contract in the first place." Charlie was speaking quietly, almost to himself, as he stared into the fire.

"How so?" Thomas asked, placing another chunk of wood on the fire. He hadn't noticed any reticence on George's part.

"Well, it seems the BIA originally expressed an interest in funding a grant to proceed with a cleanup of some of the old surface mines in an adjacent area, but as it turns out, this canyon of George's might play a key role if the program moves forward. If this cleanup is okayed, it would mean building a road nearly to the head of the creek. Much of the current site George has under survey would likely be compromised, if not eradicated entirely." Charlie looked up the trail, again lowering his voice as though he thought George Custer might still be able to hear him. "His work up there would then be considered 'salvage archaeology'. George has never been a big fan of the term, or what's involved in carrying it out. Still, he felt compelled to accept this project rather than have it move forward without proper due diligence."

Harley Ponyboy, who had been listening intently pursed his lips and had this to say; "Well, the Doc told me, this site is considered one of the last occupations in the entire area, from the end of the great migration out of this part of the country. He said there could be some valuable information here no one has yet reviewed." Harley nodded as he thought back to his conversation with the Professor. "Doc has a pretty good instinct when it comes to these things. It will be interesting to hear what he turns up." Harley had worked a good many 'digs' with George Custer—both drunk and sober—and was familiar with the man's way of thinking.

Just as Thomas was about to add his thoughts on the subject, he was interrupted by Harley standing suddenly erect and holding up a hand for quiet. He cocked his head to listen for what had escaped the other two. Closer to the noisy little fire with its cracking and popping, they had missed it. "Shhh. Surely that's not a truck engine I hear?"

The other two turned their heads toward the rough track coming into the creek bottom. Concentrating their attention in that direction, first one and then the other slowly nodded their heads.

When two points of light appeared over the last rise before the road fell off into the creek bottom, it became clear they were about to have more company.

Thinking it better to avoid waking up those in the tents, if possible, the three moved toward the parking area with Charlie in the lead, already suspecting who it might be. His earlier talk with the Professor indicated this might be a possibility but he'd still not expected a visit this soon. Not knowing if this would even happen, he'd made it a point not to mention it to the others. Tribal Policeman Billy Red Clay was the only other person who knew where they were... or how to get here. It must be something urgent for Billy to come all this way—a good bit of it in the dark of night. When the men reached their trucks, they waited as they silently watched the vehicle's slow progress. Thomas hefted himself up on the back of his flatbed with arms folded, while the other two leaned against the truck bed on either side.

Charlie was the first to break the silence. "It's Billy Red Clay," he said flatly.

"You got good eyes, *Hastinn*, I can't see a damn thing but headlights." Thomas was peering into the darkness thinking he was missing something. "What makes you think it's my Nephew?"

Harley Ponyboy looked across at Charlie and smiled in the dark. Charlie didn't make such statements without some sort of prior information. *He must have talked to the Doc earlier...* As the vehicle drew closer, a spotlight came on to check the depth of the creek crossing. "Cop-wagon all right. Who else has a spotlight?"

Harley watched as the moon shone through a rift in the clouds. "We'll know pretty quick," and then after another five minutes... "Ah, there it is... Yep, looks like Billy's rig to me."

Thomas jumped down from the truck bed and turned to glance at Charlie in the moonlight. "Smartass..." he whispered.

Billy Red Clay crossed the creek and was soon close enough to play his spotlight across the three men. He came jouncing up out of the creek bed and pulled in alongside Charlie's pickup. His SUV had barely stopped rolling before he jumped out and ran around to the passenger side, while calling to the three observers for a little help.

Thomas was first at his Nephew's side as the man opened the door and released the seatbelt on his passenger, letting him fall forward against him. The person was clearly not in control of his faculties.

Thomas quickly moved in to help remove him from the seat as Harley and Charlie stood ready to help support the person who was obviously, unable to stand on his own.

"Whatcha got here Nephew? Seems a long way to haul a drunk in the middle of the night." Thomas grimaced as he helped lift the person out.

"This boy's not drunk...he's bad hurt. We need to get him somewhere we can lay him down and see what can be done for him." Billy could see the questions in their eyes. "I'll tell you all about it later."

First one pair of helpers and then another, half-carried the boy up the hill to the camp. On the way past his truck, Charlie grabbed his first aid kit from under the seat and brought it along as well. Harley guided them to his tent and helped get the injured boy inside, laying him down on his own cot as Thomas covered him with a blanket against the evening chill. Charlie grabbed a lantern and lit it, hanging it so they could get a good look and maybe see what could be done about his wound.

"What happened to him?" Charlie asked, taking a small flashlight from his kit, and propping the boy's head to one side. Removing his hand to find it slick with blood, he declared the injury wasn't bleeding as freely as on the way up the hill. The boy's eyes were closed, and Charlie opened each in turn, shining the light into first one and then the other to get a read on his pupils. "How long has he been like this?"

Billy stood there a moment, breathing hard, trying to remember exactly how long it had been since he found him. "I'm not really sure. I was on my way out here when I found him wandering around in the middle of nowhere. He was bleeding pretty good at the time...

seemed disoriented...unable to answer questions. I knew I wasn't that far north of your camp. I was on my way out here earlier this afternoon but got turned around, trying to get my bearings. We were both lost. I first intended to get him all the way into town. Later, I recognized the turn off to this canyon and realized I was back on track to your camp, I figured it would be a lot closer to bring him here than trying to make the clinic in town." He glanced down at the boy. "There were times when he seemed a little better, even saying a few words...nothing that made any sense at the time, though."

There was a swish of a canvas flap and the men looked up to see Lucy Tallwoman and Sue Yazzie standing there wide eyed. Ida Marie Begay was craning her neck to see around them, while holding the other children back with one arm. She couldn't tear her eyes from the injured boy and moved closer for a better look. She thought he looked about her age.

Thomas spoke up, "So much for not waking everyone up." And then addressing his wife, said, "We'll be needing a pan of warm water and soap to wash this wound out along with something clean to make bandages out of."

Charlie quickly added, "Sue, I remember you saying you put some fresh T-shirts in my bag, didn't you?

Could you bring us one of those? I'm not sure what kind of bandages I'm going to have left in this kit."

Harley broke in with, "I've got a new bottle of 'blue horse lotion' in this pack box, I bought it for the mules, but it will work just as well for this. I use it on me and Harley Jr. all the time."

Charlie nodded. "Couldn't hurt. The iodine swabs that come with this kit won't work very well with a cut this size."

Lucy Tallwoman turned to Ida Marie to say, "Ida can you heat a dishpan of water? I think there's enough live embers in the fire pit to do the job."

Ida, bobbing her head, turned and was instantly gone.

Sue Yazzie pushed her way past the remaining children. "I'll get the soap and some clean washcloths." At a sign from their mother, Joseph Wiley and Sasha took a sleepy little Harley Jr. by the hand and led him, mumbling his protests to their tent and his sleeping bag.

Harley dragged up a wooden pack box for a table and after pulling out his bottle of horse medicine and opening it up, he carefully set the medical kit up on the makeshift stand. Then, reaching for a canteen of water, he held it up, asking. "Okay to give him some water?" Charlie, busy taking the boy's temperature, read the thermometer before indicating it was all right for the boy to have a drink. He then started the messy business of cleaning the head wound. Over the years, the Legal Services Investigator had taken several of the emergency medical programs offered by Health Services—as had Billy Red Clay as a requirement for his job. Billy knew Charlie had the greater experience and chose to stay back out of the way unless he needed a hand. The policeman was worn out. The entire group pitched in to help the unfortunate boy, and in very little time his head wound was cleaned and bandaged, along with a fresh shirt donated by Harley Ponyboy, who shook his head as he handed it over. He now had only one shirt left to his name. The boy was obviously feeling better now and raised his head to peer groggily around the circle of unknown but smiling faces.

Charlie and Thomas moved back to afford the patient some breathing room and were surprised when Ida Marie pushed past them with a steaming bowl of soup, she'd made it herself from a dry mix she'd found in the camp larder. Without saying a word, the girl sat herself down beside the boy's cot and began spooning the soup down him. He had obviously not eaten in some time and stared curiously at the girl as he eagerly slurped down each spoonful. Though not taking his eyes off Ida Marie even for a moment and clearly still in pain, the boy offered a wan smile of thanks. Ida Marie, for her part, hesitated only a moment before smiling back.

Harley Ponyboy nudged Thomas as the two teenagers continued to smile at one another. Lucy Tallwoman was watching as well, and appeared thoughtful for a moment, then hooked a thumb at her husband meaning it was time to turn in.

Charlie busied himself cleaning up and putting his medical kit in order, then he and Billy Red Clay, along with Harley Ponyboy, went outside where they fell to discussing the injured boy and what was to be done about him. The men convinced Billy to stay until morning and he finally agreed, saying he needed to get a deposition from the boy anyhow and that might be better left for morning. He also admitted he probably wasn't up to another long drive into town. "To tell the truth, I don't believe I'm awake enough to get back out of here in the dark anyhow, I can hardly hold my eyes open."

Harley was quick to say the Policeman could bunk in his tent with him and the boy. It would be easier, he reasoned, if there were two of them keeping an eye on their patient through the night.

Charlie nodded at all this, offering his considered opinion he thought the boy was going to be fine, all things being equal. "We can check him out in the morning again and then make a decision on what needs to be done."

Thomas and Lucy were standing by the now dead embers of the campfire, waiting for Ida Marie to come out, when the others joined them—all anxious to hear what Billy Red Clay knew of the boy, and how he came to be out there hurt and alone.

Billy didn't know quite where to start but began by saying Tribal Police had received a call the previous day from a trader, advising them of the death of a woman on an isolated part of the reservation. This was not an uncommon occurrence, and the information was passed along to Health and Human Services. Billy happened to see the report on the log that morning, but thought little of it until later, when another call came in from the same Erwin Johnson who filed the initial report. Billy said he just happened to be the one to take the call.

The man said he'd spoken to Lyla Klah's son and thought he seemed a little confused, but still was doing all right, at least in his opinion. Later, rethinking the thing, however, he decided he should at least let someone know the grief-stricken boy had struck out on his own, and by now might be in over his head. He was quick to say he'd offered to take the boy into town with him but was refused. "Maybe he was afraid of being turned over to Child Services," he said. He went on to give Billy the location of the family *hogan,* and the direction the boy indicated he would be going. He mentioned that Sam didn't seem to be thinking clearly, and that he was headed into some pretty rough country for someone his age.

Billy said he took down Johnson's information, including where he lived, and then belatedly asked if he was a relative of the boy. Erwin hesitated a moment but said, "No, just an old friend of the family."

Billy, after thinking it over, took the report to the Captain, who decided it might be a good idea to take a run out there and check with both the trader and this Erwin Johnson. The Captain liked Billy and knew how hard he'd been working of late—figured a drive in the country might be just the thing on so pretty a day.

The young Officer went on with his story. "The trading post was right on the way to Johnson's place, so I stopped to have a little chat with him first. The trader said it was a sad case; the woman had been in declining health for some time, and he had already allowed them more credit on their account than he normally would. Still, he knew they were low on food, and eventually carried their account right up to woman's death. He said she would only take the bare necessities and that both she and her son must have gone hungry a lot of the time."

Charlie had a question. "So, you checked in with the trader before talking to this Erwin Johnson, and decided to go looking for the boy instead?"

"Yes, after talking to the trader, I thought I might come up here and gather up some help to look for the boy. It wasn't long after that I missed your turn off and got turned around. That was when I found him. I figured Erwin Johnson could wait—as it turns out I'm glad I did—any longer and that boy might have been in real trouble."

Charlie thought he was right. "The boy was in a bad way for sure. Any later and you might have missed him in the dark. A night laying out in the cold bleeding, could have made for a different ending to this story." Charlie then nodded, saying, "In the morning, he may be up to explaining how he came to be in this mess. Was he able to tell you his name?"

"No, he was never able to say anything, but the trader said the dead woman's son was named Sam Klah and gave me a pretty good description. I'm fairly certain this is who we have here. If he's not well enough to talk by morning, I thought maybe Harley could go back up there with me and help back-track him to see if we can find out what happened."

Thomas edged into the conversation. "That might be a good idea. Charlie and I can take Harley's mules up and pack out some of Doc Custer's stuff...at least get one good load out, before you boys get back. Then we can go from there."

Harley said this would work for him and told Billy Red Clay he'd be willing to do whatever he could to help. Yawning, he then said, "It looks to me like we should all be getting some sleep. I expect there'll be plenty for everyone to do tomorrow."

Ida Marie Begay was just coming out of Harley's tent and proceeded to walk right past the little gathering as though they weren't even there. Lucy Tallwoman reached out and touched her arm. "So, how is he, Ida?"

Ida Marie stopped and gave her an odd look, saying, "Why, he's much better, he's going to be just fine. His name is Sam and he's almost exactly the same age as me."

Thomas watched his daughter go to their tent and turning to his wife groaned, "Tell me this isn't what I think it is!"

Lucy suppressed a smile, "I've heard of this 'first sight' stuff but never really believed in it... She's never really shown much interest in boys before, but this one seems to have caught her eye."

Charlie smiling, replied, "Maybe it's the Florence Nightingale syndrome. You know, where the nurse falls in love with the patient?"

"That's what I am afraid of," Thomas growled as he motioned his wife toward their tent.

Charlie was grinning as he left the group. He would have a lot to tell Sue come morning.

Chapter 5

The Question

The morning following the arrival of the injured Sam Klah, Tribal Officer Billy Red Clay visited the boy, who was then able to give a halting account of his recent efforts to find his Uncle. The Tribal Policeman listened closely to the part about how he was attacked from behind by someone he never saw or heard coming. The Tribal Officer took special note of the boy's obviously weakened condition. Then, sensing his reluctance to leave the company of these people, decided against hauling him into town until he could speak to Charlie about it.

After listening to Billy, Charlie Yazzie quickly agreed, saying it might well be best he stay with them until he felt better. The Navajo Cop now convinced this option might be the better way to proceed agreed to leave Sam Klah in his friends' care, at least until he could get in touch with his superiors for an official ruling in the matter.

Billy took leave of the camp, telling the Legal Services Investigator, as soon as he could find some decent radio-reception, he would call in to let his Captain know he'd found Sam Klah, and make him aware of the boy's story. He would also let the Captain know, since he was already in the area, he would be heading back to Erwin Johnson's place before returning to the office. He would say he wanted to clear up a few questions about the mother's death. What he really wanted was a line on the whereabouts of the boy's uncle, and whether or not the man would be willing to take Sam in, if only until a more permanent place could be found for him.

~~~~~~

Later in the morning, Charlie Yazzie, giving the boy enough time to collect his thoughts, waited a moment or two before announcing himself at the tent flap. Sam answered and Charlie went in voicing some pleasantry in Navajo as he pulled up a chair. "So, you are the notorious Sam Klah." He smiled at his attempt to inject a little humor.

Sam propped himself up on one elbow, as he attempted to focus on his visitor, then had to immediately put out a hand to balance himself—The boy grimaced at the flash of light in his throbbing head. He said softly, "Yes, that's me all right, but right now I wish it wasn't."

Charlie chuckled, "I can understand that...you took quite a rap on the head, but you're young and will likely get past this rather quickly. It may hurt for a few days and there's the possibility you may experience some headaches...maybe for some time." He reached in his shirt pocket for a small envelope of tablets. "Here's some aspirin to help with that, one, or even two, if it seems bad. That should fix it. He shook out a couple of pills and, reaching over to the pack box for a water bottle, handed it to the boy to wash down the tablets.

Sam eased his legs off the cot and set up to take the aspirin in a gulp. "Thank you," he said in English. "I heard someone say last night that you are with Tribal's Legal Services?"

"That's right. I'm Investigator Charlie Yazzie. My family and some of our friends happened to be on a camping trip out here when Officer Red Clay brought you in last night." He paused a moment to hand the boy his card then said, "Billy thought you might not be up to traveling this morning and might be better off right here with us for a day or two. He had the impression you were not interested in being referred to Child Services." Charlie frowned when he said this. "Despite what you may have heard, those people are dedicated professionals and would do their best to help you, Sam." He realized he might be coming across as trying to convince the boy this was his only option and laughed, partially at the look on the boy's face, but mainly at himself. "I'm sure that's a choice you can deal with yourself, on down the road. If you should come around to thinking that's an option, we can discuss it further. No one here is going to push you in that direction, I promise."

There was another idea in the back of Charlie's mind, one he thought might provide yet another avenue for the young man. He would have to give it a little more thought before sounding the boy out, but it might well turn out to be a real opportunity for the young man.

Sam, still appearing lost in thought, looked doubtful, then dropping his eyes to the floor, said. "I can take care of myself once I get back on my feet, Mr. Yazzie. When I find my uncle, I'm sure he'll want to help me."

"Sam, you've never even met the man and still have no idea where he lives...at least not from what I've heard."

"I can find him."

Charlie nodded, "Well, you may have some help with that, Officer Red Clay will be looking into your uncle's whereabouts, starting first thing this morning. He'll let us know as soon as he hears something. You can hang out here for a couple of days and get to feeling better. If Billy does find your uncle, I'll see that you are the first to know." He paused a moment and smiled to let the boy know he was on his side. "In the meantime, you're welcome to join in on our little camping vacation."

The boy nodded at this, expressing his gratitude with a slow grin. "There is something I'd like to know." He said. "If you would tell me?" Charlie nodded. "Which of your friends is the girl's father...that girl Ida Marie who helped me when I was first brought here?"

Charlie cocked his head to one side and considered the young man. "That would be Thomas Begay, the tall man in the black hat. Why do you ask?"

The boy slowly stood up then, holding a cautious hand to his bandaged head, he steadied himself at the edge of the bed. Looking directly at the Investigator he declared in no uncertain terms, "Well...the thing is, I intend to marry her."

Charlie laughed, thinking the boy was joking. But quickly realizing he was serious, instantly changed expression. Pursing his lips and gesturing toward the tent flap he grew thoughtful. "I see... Well, I've known Thomas for a good many years. Maybe you should let me sound him out on the idea first?" Then on an impulse. "Have you mentioned this to Ida Marie?"

"Not yet, I haven't, but I will as soon as I see her this morning."

"Just a thought, but do you think it might be a good idea to get a little better acquainted before you spring something like this on her?"

"Oh no, she has already come to me in a dream last night. She agreed we should be married."

Charlie smiled at this. "Things sometimes look a little different to a woman in the light of day...they have been known to change their minds you know, and sometimes without any real reason, as far as the average man can see." The Legal Services Investigator had some experience dealing with the more isolated people on the Reservation and was now aware this boy came from a very traditional and isolated upbringing. Even so, this talk of marrying Ida Marie was a little more than he was prepared for. *Maybe that thump on his head made the boy a little delusional.* Hopefully, though, it was just a passing glitch in his thinking. He might still come to his senses and listen to reason, in time.

Charlie realized there was someone who might know a little more about Sam Klah's line of reasoning. Harley Ponyboy was from that part of the country and had grown up in much the same circumstances as the boy, and Charlie hoped he might have an idea how to handle things.

He knew the girl's father considered himself a traditionalist as well but was equally sure the boy's idea of a spur-of-the-moment marriage proposal would not go down well with the man. No, not with him, or with Lucy Tallwoman, both of whom had big plans for Ida Marie. They realized early on how bright the girl was, exceptionally bright they thought, and ambitious along with it. They would certainly want more for the girl than this boy, with so few prospects—no matter how taken with him she might be.

On the other hand, Ida Marie's brother Caleb, was likely to be more in tune with the idea of her getting married and moving out. Charlie suspected Caleb held the notion his big sister still considered him under her supervision. Now that he had a girlfriend of his own, he would probably welcome the thought of Ida Marie getting married. It was hard for Charlie to get his mind around how fast all these kids were growing up...including his own. Generally, everyone in a Navajo family gets a chance to be heard in such things. Only old Paul T'Sosi would be the unknown. To Charlie's way of thinking the inscrutable old man might go either way. He'd long been an advocate for the girl even from the time she'd first come to them. He was old enough to remember how these things were once handled.

~~~~~~

In the meantime, Sam Klah had sat himself back down on his cot to ponder the idea of this man from Legal Services acting as a go-between, for Ida Marie and himself. Tilting his head to one side, he slowly nodded and then smiled as he studied Charlie's card. *This person was obviously right. This was, indeed, the proper way to go about it. He would absolutely need someone to represent him to the family going forward. Who better than Thomas Begay's best friend to present his case?* Surely this was an omen. His own mother had married quite young, his father's uncle presenting the case for the young man. It had been common enough back in that time. Surely there should be no problem with this marriage going forward.

Charlie Yazzie and Sam Klah sat a moment each with his own perception of how things would likely play out, and each without a clue how far off their thinking would eventually prove to be.

Charlie was first to speak. "Well, then, I'll just go find Thomas Begay and see what he has to say to your proposal....see which way the wind blows...if you know what I mean?"

The Boy nodded eagerly, beaming now that the thing was about to be settled.

Chapter. 6

The Suspect

Billy's Tribal unit sat alongside the highway while the Policeman leafed through his notes from the trader, refreshing his overview of Erwin Johnson before he spoke with him again. His first encounter with the man, came when Erwin reported young Sam Klah's dilemma, and the death of his mother. There still was a bit of doubt in Billy's mind, as to how the man fit into the lives of Sam and his mother. His recent phone conversation with Erwin had left Billy with a vague feeling of unease. What this person deemed an act of charitable duty, left the young officer unconvinced. There seemed to be more involved than just a distant neighbor's gesture of concern. Running Erwin's name through his own agency's, admittedly poor, data base, he came up with nothing to justify these suspicions. Billy's position as Liaison Officer to the FBI did, of course, offer the option of having the feds run a more comprehensive check, but the fact was, he had no real evidence to warrant the request, not at this stage of the game anyway. Billy Red Clay had never been one to ask for help until he had exhausted all of his own resources, even more so when it came to asking Senior FBI Agent Fred Smith for help. He doubted he'd been in his current position long enough to warrant such a favor.

Billy looked up to the Bureau as the ultimate law enforcement agency, and had once secretly considered applying for admittance to the academy at Quantico. Agent Fred Smith, himself, had once mentioned he thought Billy would make a fine agent, and that he would be willing to put in a good word for him to that effect. Billy had never forgotten the comment, and though he pushed the thought to the back of his mind, it resurfaced occasionally despite his best efforts.

~~~~~

Erwin Johnson's doublewide turned out to be in a secluded back canyon with no near neighbors evident. Billy pulled into the yard to the barking of a friendly looking dog who trotted alongside all the way to the front door.

Stepping down from his vehicle, Billy tugged his hat a little lower and stepped onto the wooden porch, pausing a moment for a final look around. The place appeared neat and well-kept, though lacking any effort at landscaping, beyond the two struggling young cottonwood saplings on either side of the path to the door. Even this slight effort, however, showed some sense of pride in the residence, at least to Billy's way of thinking. Certainly, the place was better kept than many in the area.

The dog didn't come onto the porch, satisfying himself with sitting beside the front step, head cocked to one side in anticipation. Billy's first impression of Erwin's place was at odds with his previous opinion of the man. He hesitated a moment, trying to sort this out.

Knocking on the door, Billy thought he should have at least given a beep of his horn just to alert anyone inside they had company. It was considered a common curtesy in that country, almost obligatory actually, and Billy was momentarily uncertain why he had failed to do so. It was a lawman's prerogative, of course, to employ the element of surprise when thought warranted, this despite it not aligning with Navajo tradition. A Tribal officer often walked a thin line when it came to traditional mores, versus modern law enforcement training.

Erwin Johnson came to the door disheveled, looking as though he might have woken from a nap. He was a big man with a big man's bluster, but immediately toned this down as he took in Billy's uniform and the official Tribal unit parked in the yard.

"Yes? How can I help you?" His voice, educated and self-assured, was somehow not as the Tribal Officer remembered it from the man's earlier phone report. He was, in fact, not at all what Billy expected and he continued looking him up and down before answering, "Mr. Erwin Johnson?"

The man nodded shortly.

Billy thought he detected some uneasiness in his manner, though the man's expression remained calm and self-assured enough.

"I'm Officer Billy Red Clay, Tribal Police. I took your report on the death of Sam Klah's mother Lyla Klah." He paused long enough to give Erwin ample opportunity to reply. When that didn't happen, he moved on as though he hadn't noticed. "At the time of your call you seemed to feel the boy's leaving home to find his uncle might be more than he could handle. I would like to talk to you about that for a moment, if I might?"

The big man considered this, offering what might be taken for a smile. "Sure, I remember talking to you, officer." Johnson offered his hand and shook with a firm grip. "Come on in the house and sit down, I'll put some coffee on. I could use a cup myself."

Inside Billy found the house to be plainly furnished but clean and comfortable looking, certainly a cut above the reservation norm. Following the man into the kitchen, he took the chair his host indicated and sat back to study the man.

Erwin, seeming not to notice, moved to the stove and began putting together a pot of coffee. "So, what can I tell you about Sam and Lyla Klah? I've known them both for some years... Sam since he was born. I suppose I know as much about them as anyone."

Billy was struck by the man's straightforward manner of speaking—obviously educated to a degree he hadn't expected there in the back country. He couldn't remember the man's speech being quite so cultured at the time of the report but thought perhaps Johnson's concern at the time might have been the cause.

Billy, abruptly changed the direction of the interview, casually asking, "Do you live here alone Erwin—not married? No children?"

Erwin laughed as he brought cups and spoons to the table. "No, no, not married, no children. I used to have a place in town, but after my parents passed away, I took their place over. I've lived here, by myself, for years now...maybe too long, but I've pretty much gotten used to it." He pushed the sugar bowl and a miniature pitcher of creamer to Billy's side of the table. Then he sat down to wait for the coffee to perk, eyeing the policeman with a mild curiosity.

Billy Red Clay opened his notebook and began scribbling in it. He had picked up his method of interviewing from an FBI seminar he'd once attended—moving quickly from one question, to an unrelated one, or one out of sequence, all designed to throw a subject off guard. The man's manner of speaking reminded the young Officer of Charlie Yazzie when he first came home from the University.

Johnson yawned and looked over at the coffee pot as though to hurry it along.

Billy lay down his pen and, looking up, sighed. "Seems like we were both up late last night." He narrowed an eye at Erwin and touched the tip of his tongue to his upper lip. "I found Sam Klah...just before dark last night...wandering along an abandoned mine road west of here. He was badly hurt and seemed disoriented when I spotted him. I was pretty much lost myself at the time—it was only by luck that I found him at all—another few hours and things might have gone badly for him." He thought he saw a flicker of surprise at this but couldn't be sure. It might have been the coffee pot boiling that signaled the man to rise quickly and return to the stove. Billy's hand dropped unseen to the weapon at his hip and then back to the table and his notebook as the man turned from the stove with the coffee. "You wouldn't have any idea how he wound up out there would you Erwin?"

The man went gimlet eyed and with a slight curl of his lip raised his voice, saying, "No, I wouldn't have the *slightest* idea." He sat the pot down. "So, is the boy in the hospital now, or what? I warned him it could be dangerous for a stranger alone in that country." He looked away quickly but in only a moment had gathered himself. "Did the hospital think he was going to be all right?"

"He's not in a hospital Mr. Johnson...I left him with friends up in Spring Creek, where he can be cared for until he's recovered enough to move. I'll be checking on him from time to time. Investigator Yazzie from Legal Services and his family are up there on a camping trip, they're with him now. Charlie seems to think he'll be much better in a day or so."

Johnson gave the Police Officer an odd look, one meant to betray nothing yet speaking volumes.

Changing the subject, Billy casually asked. "How well did you know Sam Klah's Uncle?"

Erwin gave a trivializing shake of his head yet drew back slightly, seemingly surprised at the question. "I grew up with John and Lyla, from the time we were all children."

"In your opinion, would he be a good person for the boy to find shelter with?"

"I wouldn't want to say, it's really none of my business who the boy goes to."

"Well then do you have any idea where I might locate Mr. Etcitty?"

"I haven't spoken to the man in years. I suppose he could be anywhere, but somewhere here on the reservation most likely. He would be out of his element anywhere else."

Billy Red Clay nodded slightly at this. "I see. Well, in that case, I expect this should about cover what I needed to know." Then looking down at his notes, surprised Erwin with, "Oh...one last thing. It's been reported you offered to move in with the boy's mother...after his father's death...is that correct?"

Erwin, taking a moment to answer, sounded a bit uncertain, as though unsure if he should answer at all. Finally, he said, "I don't know who told you that...it was a long time ago. As I said, we grew up together and after her husband's death I may have felt sorry for her. I did spend some time there, but she later decided she didn't want me to move in with her and the boy and I stopped coming around. That was about the size of it I guess."

Erwin lifted the still steaming coffee pot from its ceramic trivet, pouring them both cups, which they proceeded to doctor with cream and sugar before sipping the brew under an almost palpable veil of silence.

Pushing back his cup finally, Billy thanked the man saying, "Mr. Johnson. I appreciate you talking with me this morning, and should you hear anything you think might help us find the boy's uncle, please don't hesitate to be in touch with us." Billy turned as he rose from his chair. "You understand, Erwin, I might have further questions as time goes on and may be in touch again."

Johnson nodded grimly and followed the Officer to the door without another word. Going back in the kitchen, Erwin went over the interview in his mind and decided there really wasn't anything to be concerned about. This young cop was clearly on a fishing expedition but had come up with nothing in the slightest that should worry him.

Outside Billy sat in his car staring at the closed door of the house for several minutes, making a few additional notations in his book. There was a lot more to this Erwin Johnson than met the eye. *What was an obviously well-educated man doing living out here by himself, how did he make his living...and what was his backstory?* Billy thought now, he might in fact have to call on Agent

Smith, if only for a more complete picture of who this man was. *What was Johnson's game?*

Chapter 7

The Dig

Charlie Yazzie was supervising the unpacking of yet another collection of Professor Custer's fragile specimens—those entrusted to Harley Ponyboy's better natured mules. George Custer was inside his horse trailer filling the wooden packing boxes with straw for the long trip into town and checking his inventory list as the items came in.

"We haven't had a single damaged piece yet." George was elated and it showed in his satisfied smile. "There were some fine pieces left for us to recover...far beyond my expectations. I have you boys to thank for getting these things out in such good condition."

Thomas Begay grinned as he carried in an especially well-preserved black on white drinking mug, cradling it carefully with both hands. "Yep, so far, so good. I would guess that portion of the overhang that sloughed off back in ancient times, is what saved a lot of this stuff from the pot hunters. The harder it was to get to, the less likely it was they would take the time."

"You're right there, and I was lucky a seismic crew was finishing their work up on top. They were good enough to bring down a couple of hydraulic jacks to shift those slabs over the edge. Otherwise, we would have had to wait for the road crew and their heavy equipment. That would have put a lot more pressure on us. Even with a good operator, the big machines often destroy about as much as they save. Luck was on our side this time, for sure. I was happy to have your gang up there helping today, that saved a lot of time."

Thomas chuckled. "The girls and the kids had a great time up there, Doc. You know how to keep their attention, I'll say that. I'm sure you saw Lucy taking notes for the next meeting of the Tribal Council. Your talk about the people who lived up there left quite an impression on her. She seemed to think it was information that would come in handy at future Council meetings." He smiled his satisfaction. "When the question of Tribal involvement in the protection of these sites comes up again, you can bet she'll be ready."

Custer nodded. "I'm glad they enjoyed it; God knows it's been long enough since I've had anyone to lecture to. I hoped they would get something out of it."

Charlie had come to the trailer door with the last box of the more breakable items. "I think everyone got a lot out of it, Doc. Sam Klah seemed especially interested. He's a smart boy from what I've seen, with a lot of potential, should he get a little nudge in the right direction."

Thomas Begay turned to his friend, frowning at the mention of the boy's name. "That Kid's got a lot of nerve sending you to talk to me about Ida Marie. He better be glad he didn't come in person!"

"I sort 'a figured... That's why I offered to pave the way." Charlie was grinning as he brushed past the frowning Thomas to set his box down with a flourish. "George, remind me to tell you what our friend here said when I told him Sam wanted to marry his daughter."

Thomas shook his head and scowled as he went back out to unsaddle the mules.

George Custer watched him go then, with a lowered eyelid asked, "What did he say, Charlie?"

Laughing, Charlie answered as he caught his breath. "Well, he was eating breakfast and didn't even look up...didn't bat an eye. I just told him straight up that Sam Klah sent me to ask for his daughter's hand in marriage—just like that."

The professor was smiling too now, anticipating a good joke on Thomas who he'd known for years, quite aware that the man was a trickster himself. He also knew Thomas had a temper when the joke was on him.

Charlie snorted, "Doc, he didn't miss a beat. He said, calm as could be, 'It will cost him twenty head of good horses and fifty sheep,' like it was a hundred years ago. He'd thought I was joking, of course and wouldn't let on it bothered him. It was all I could do to keep a straight face, but I did…never cracked a smile. When I didn't answer him, he began coming around to the fact that I wasn't just messing with him."

George Custer's eyes went wide "And then what?"

"Well, I told him that seemed a high price, even for a girl as nice as Ida Marie, and that I doubted the boy could come up with it. I let him know Sam only had two horses to his name and didn't know where they were at the moment. Run off or stolen most likely."

The professor was holding a hand to his mouth, leaning on a packing crate, laughing as a tear rolled down his cheek. "So, then you told him the truth?"

"No, Doc, I'd already told him the truth, Sam Klah said he intends to marry Ida Marie no matter what—that's the truth."

The Professor had a blank look on his face as he mulled this over. "He'll kill him, won't he?"

Charlie shot his old Professor a sharp look. "Not if I can help it, George. That's why I sent Sam along with you and the others up to the dig—and asked Harley Ponyboy to go along just to provide a little extra protection—he's the only one who can handle Thomas when he blows up. He can be unpredictable, as you well know. As for the boy, he's as green as a gourd, Doc. He doesn't realize what he's done, but he will soon enough. I was going to give you a heads up when you first brought the mules down, but never got the chance. Sue knows what's going on and said she'd make sure everyone took their time hiking back down from the dig. Maybe give Thomas a chance to cool off."

George had stopped smiling, and was, in fact, looking rather worried. "I hope I haven't put you folks in a bad situation. It's my fault you're all up here in the first place."

"Not at all, George. Thomas has cooled down a good bit since morning and, if I know him, he's already beginning to see the humor in the thing himself. Let's hope so anyway."

~~~~~

Thomas Begay was measuring out a bait of oats to the mules when he suddenly cocked his head toward the canyon rim. After a moment he called to the two men finishing up in the trailer. "Did you two hear a shot just now?"

Charlie Yazzie came to the door wiping the dust off his hands. "What was that?"

"I said, did you hear a shot just now? Sounded like a long gun to me, a big caliber, too. None of our bunch has anything like that. Harley might have taken his revolver, but it wasn't a pistol I heard."

Charlie turned his head toward the upper end of the canyon and listened along with Thomas.

Doc Custer was right behind, frowning as he turned in the same direction. "No one's been shooting during all the time I've been up here. There's no hunting season open that I'm aware of either."

Thomas held up a hand. "Listen! Sounds like people shouting...kids yelling... We better get up there." He grabbed one of the mules by its lead rope and swung aboard bareback, kicking the surprised animal to a trot then into a high lope as he hit the creek bottom and started up the canyon trail.

Charlie and George stared at one another for an instant, then broke into a run themselves. Charlie quickly outdistanced the Professor as he tried to keep Thomas in sight, seeing him pull his mule to a halt in a cloud of dust and swing off, hitting the ground running. The mule, not comfortable being left behind, was right at his heels, neck stretched and braying at the top of his lungs. Hearing a rattle of gravel, Charlie saw Lucy Tallwoman and Ida Marie sliding down a steep game path to the main trail. Not far behind, Joseph Wiley came dragging his sister by one hand, skidding down the rocky path in a flurry of dust. Bringing up the rear, Sue Yazzie was barely able to keep her balance as she dragged the squalling whirlwind that was "little Harley" by one arm. There was no sign of Harley Ponyboy, or Sam Klah.

Thomas reached the frightened group in time to take the breathless Lucy Tallwoman by the arm as she slewed off the steep edge of the trail with Ida Marie at her side.

"Someone took a shot at Sam on our way down here!" the girl screeched, twisting her head to glance back up the trail. She was almost bowled over by Charlie's son and daughter who were coming full tilt behind her.

Lucy, completely out of breath now, was trying to explain as best she was able. "Harley took off after the shooter with his pistol. We couldn't keep Sam Klah from running after him." Out of wind, she leaned over to catch her breath.

Sue Yazzie, equally winded, was nonetheless quick to assure them no one had been hurt. "That bullet barely missed Sam's head... Knocked the bark off a tree right next to him!"

Thomas turned to Charlie, who was busy making sure that everyone was, indeed, all right. "We better get after Harley, you know how he is when he gets his dander up—there's no stopping him. He's a little under-gunned to take on someone with a rifle."

Charlie nodded, holding up a hand and taking a deep breath said. "Okay. Let's go." He then yelled back over his shoulder to the Professor, who was just now panting his way up to the group. "Doc, stay down here with the women, they might need some help, should the shooter circle back. Try to keep everyone under cover!" He figured the girls were aware they should hunker down until the situation was resolved and, knowing George Custer was in no shape to join the chase, thought it best for everyone concerned the professor should stay behind.

Thomas, already in the act of catching up the loose mule, found it had now reconsidered its options and was staying just out of reach. Eventually securing a grip on the lead rope, Thomas began their scramble up the steep path to the much easier main trail. Charlie had a hard time catching them but, with a determined burst of effort managed to take hold of the mule's tail, making it easier to keep up. When they hit the upper trail, Thomas jumped on the mule and offered Charlie a hand up. "You better get up behind me. It's still a ways to the top. If we are going to catch up to Harley and that crazy kid this mule can save us some time."

Charlie, still gasping to catch his breath, didn't argue. It was a good size mule and, he thought, had proven itself gentle enough to accept an additional rider.

Keeping the animal to a fast trot, they hadn't gone much more than a mile when they spotted Harley Ponyboy headed their way through an open sage flat. He looked worn out. Thomas reined the mule aside to meet him, whispering over his shoulder, "Harley wouldn't be out in the open like that if he thought the shooter was anywhere around. That no-good must have high-tailed it."

They could see no sign of Sam Klah.

"Where's the boy?" was the first words out of Charlie Yazzie's mouth, as they came within speaking distance.

Harley had his big frame Colt .38 stuck in his belt, and one glance told them it wasn't going to be good news.

Harley spit dust and sage pollen out the side of his mouth and with a grimace wiped his face on his sleeve. "I tried to get Sam to go back down and get help, but he wouldn't. He said he was the one who got shot at, and that he intended to find out for himself who did it. When we topped out the rim I found where the bastard took the shot and tracked him for a short distance before finding where he'd left a horse. When I showed Sam the tracks, he took one look and said, 'that looks like my horse. He's a little cow hocked and puts one rear foot down funny.' Then, before I could stop him, the boy bolted out in front on a dead run. I couldn't catch him. He yelled back from the top of the next rise that he could see someone on horseback down country. From what I could make out, the boy was sure it was his horse the man was riding." Harley shook his head, his frustration, and exhaustion showing in the grim set of his jaw, and the defeated look he gave them. "When I tried to call him back. He wouldn't come, just waved, and took off again. I knew there was no chance he'd catch the bastard, him without a horse and all. One thing I will say, the boy's tough as a boot, and has grit to spare, I'll give him that much." Harley shook his head sadly. "That young man has no idea what he's letting himself in for—going off on his own like this, and unarmed, too. I seriously doubt he can catch the man, but I know now he's the kind that doesn't give up. I expect anything could happen now."

Thomas listened to all this with eyes flashing. "I'll go after him! I might be able to catch him on this mule."

Charlie put a hand on his arm. "I think it would be better to let Harley have this mule back and let him go after them—he's the tracker, he's got a gun. Besides it's his mule."

Smiling, Harley reached for the lead rope, and said, "You boys go back down and get yourself a couple of horses, and you might want to throw some food and blankets on another mule. This could get real interesting before it's over." Without another word the little man mounted up and was gone.

Thomas glared after him and frowned at Charlie as they turned for camp. "I imagine I could have caught up to that crazy-ass boy as quick as Harley could."

Charlie just smiled. "I doubt it. No one can track like Harley, and no one can get as much out of a mule as he can. We both know that." He took a deep breath and then, ignoring his friend's dark mood, started back for camp.

~~~~~

Professor Custer was first to meet them coming off the hill. "Couldn't find them...?"

Thomas looked away as Charlie answered. "We found Harley and he's going after Sam now. Thomas and I will catch up to them and we'll go from there. We could be gone for a couple of days, should things play out the way I suspect." He put a hand on the Professor's shoulder. "What I'd like for you to do, George, if you will, is gather everyone up and see they get back to town. This has turned into more than we bargained for. It's far too dangerous for the families to stay up here now." He stopped and thought a moment before going on. "And, if you will, could you get in touch with Billy Red Clay and let him know what's going on?"

The Professor was nodding as he listened, and when Charlie finished speaking, assured him he would take care of everything. Charlie watched as the man gathered everyone together and leading them aside, began explaining what the plan was now—that they would have to break camp and leave for home as quickly as possible.

The Investigator suspected his longtime mentor would be right back up here as soon as he had the others safe at home, but hoped Sue could change his mind. He and Thomas saddled two of the horses, and a pack mule, bringing along a horse for Sam Klah as well, for when they found him. If they found him.

Chapter 8

The Conundrum

As soon as he returned from his interview with Erwin Johnson, Billy Red Clay called Senior Agent Fred Smith and asked him to run the man through their system in Albuquerque. When the FBI man called back it was to say he'd better come to the office so they could go over the report together. The Navajo Cop took this to mean he'd found something...out of the ordinary. Billy Red Clay sat with a stunned look on his face as he listened to what the Bureau had managed to dig up on Johnson.

Fred ran his hand through his thinning hair, pausing a moment to see what effect the new information was having, and saw Billy was having a hard time getting his head around it. He waited for it to sink in and then continued reading the report. Billy now seemed lost in thought as he occasionally raised his head to study the FBI man. He couldn't help noticing how nearly bald Fred had become. The Agent had often mentioned the hardest part of his job was the wear and tear on his head. Damned if he wasn't right.

Finally, Fred passed the folder across the desk to Billy and watched as he ran his finger along the highlighted portions. Laying the report back on the desk, he asked in a small voice, "Fred are you sure you have the right guy? It's hard to believe this Johnson character, living alone out in the middle of nowhere, once worked for Legal Services."

"Believe it, Billy. The information is correct, We checked, and cross checked. It's him all right."

"So, I'm assuming this was back before Charlie Yazzie came on board over at Legal?"

"Yes, it was when Pete Fish was still the office manager, and one of the most corrupt periods that particular agency ever experienced. Charlie actually came in some time after Pete took over. Erwin Johnson was already gone a while by then. I was still attached to the Albuquerque office at the time, but I recall the Bureau

Agent in charge here was involved up to his eyebrows in the scandal, along with several high-up Council members." He ran a finger along his own notes as though to verify the timeline involved. "The murder of a Sioux woman named Patsy Greyhorse was the catalyst that finally brought down the entire bunch. The BIA doesn't take kindly to having one of their people knocked off in the pursuit of her duty—even though she was, most likely, as dirty as the rest. Funny how those people think, huh?" Fred's face darkened. "Our office in Albuquerque was plenty embarrassed by the Agent's part in the sad affair. I'm sure you've heard how Charlie Yazzie and your Uncle Thomas had a hand in bringing him down. That Agent was the only person I ever heard of Charlie shooting. Self-defense, of course. He and Thomas were both totally exonerated. Charlie's work on the case was thought to be the defining factor in his later rise through the ranks at Legal Services."

Billy nodded, smiling. "I was still in High School back then, but everyone in town was talking about the Patsy Greyhorse murder, and being as how Thomas is my Uncle, I paid particular attention. In fact, those stories were part of the reason I later put in my application at Tribal Police."

Fred smiled, remembering when he first met the young Officer and how far he had come since that time. "Well, I'm glad you did. We've enjoyed working with you." The FBI man leafed through the report as he pursed his lips in thought. "Getting back to Erwin Johnson, he was apparently heading up the records section over at Legal back then—one of the few higher-ups Federal Prosecutors didn't bring charges against. There were rumors he might be involved in something but they couldn't tie him to the case they were working on. Some thought Johnson saw what was coming and was smart enough to get out before it all hit the fan. There were those in the Prosecutor's office who felt he warranted a second look, but the man had already dropped out of sight, and their hands were full enough as it was. Long after the thing was over, an audit of his former office turned up missing, along with his personal file folders. Until now, his name doesn't come up again in *our* files until he reported the death of Sam's mother, Lyla Klah, and mentioned that her teenage son had struck out on his own."

Well," Billy said, his mind already awash with questions, "I suppose that explains Johnson's obvious education, and maybe even why he's kept a low profile in his later years. What it doesn't explain is how he gets along out there. Where does he get his money?"

"I suppose that's a question that deserves an answer as well. Maybe Investigator Yazzie can shed some light on that when he gets back. Charlie knows a lot of the old timer's over there at Legal. Maybe there's someone still there who has some information to share."

Billy sat back in his chair, his neck hurt, and he turned his head till something popped, and then after repeating this in the other direction, he blinked and returned his gaze to the FBI man. "There *might* be someone at Legal who knows something, and will admit to it, but that's got to be a long shot after all these years. The *Diné* don't often implicate other people even to Navajo lawmen, as you well know."

With a silent nod, Fred admitted this was, unfortunately, the case, adding, "Still, it's worth a try."

Billy reluctantly agreed and brightened slightly as he recalled making an additional request. "What about the inquiry into Sam Klah's Uncle? Were you able to turn up anything on that guy?"

Fred Smith leaned forward and, spreading his hands flat on the desk, declared softly, "Not a Damn thing, Billy. We have absolutely nothing on John Etcitty. Not his whereabouts or personal information of any kind. Nothing. We don't even know when or where he was born." The Agent pushed his chair back from the desk, clasping his hands behind his head. "It's like he never existed. I know there are a good many undocumented people running under the radar out there on the reservation, but this is the most remarkable instance I've run into lately. Our office can generally dig up *something* on nearly anyone, but not this time." Fred was a little puzzled at this himself. "We'll keep poking around, of course, but I have to tell you, I think we've already taken our best shot. Unless you can turn up something further from your own people, we may be at a standstill on this one."

~~~~~~

Billy Red Clay was half-way back to his office when it occurred to him that he'd just passed Lucy Tallwoman's truck going the other direction. He'd been under the impression that she and Sue Yazzie weren't due back from the camping trip for several days yet. Looking in the rearview mirror, he saw she had obviously seen him as well and was now pulling over, waving from a half-lowered window, and shouting something he couldn't hear.

Billy whipped his unit around and pulled in behind her pick-up, noticing a jumble of camping gear in the back as he made his way to the front of the vehicle.

Lucy rolled her window down the rest of the way and, with a worried look on her face, launched into a torrent of words.

The Navajo Cop, having a hard time understanding, threw up his hands. "Whoa, slow down. I can't make out a word you're saying."

The woman grew quiet, as she raised her eyes skyward and took a deep breath. Regaining her composure to some extent, she was able to say, "Sorry, Billy, I was just on my way to find you. Professor Custer probably has a call into you by now, too. I wanted to be sure you knew everything going on up at the camp."

Ida Marie, looking around her Stepmother from the passenger seat and obviously worried, could do little more than bob her head up and down, unable to get a single word into the fast-paced conversation.

Billy had never seen his Uncle's wife so upset. The normally collected woman seemed barely able to contain herself.

What with Billy's continuing questions, Lucy's disjointed report took some time to tell. Even then, the Tribal Cop struggled to understand the full sequence of events at the camp.

The Officer, finally holding up a calming hand, once again assured the woman he would immediately make certain there was a bulletin out to local law enforcement. He was sure George Custer would have already reported the incident to the Farmington officials, but would check with Fred to make certain the FBI was in the loop.

~~~~~~

The Policeman was already back in his office, and on the phone, when he realized *he* himself might have been the source of the information regarding Sam Klah's whereabouts. *If Erwin Johnson is actually involved in this attempt on the boy's life, it may have been my fault someone knew where to find him. Stupid, stupid, stupid.*

Pulling the topo maps for Spring Creek Canyon Billy winced at the rugged terrain. *It's Country like this that makes it easy to get lost, and even harder to be found. It's no wonder I got turned around out there. It's a miracle I ran across Sam Klah at all.*

The Policeman spent the next few minutes convincing his Captain they needed to send someone out to the scene of the shooting. Should this unknown assailant manage to evade his Uncle and the others, the situation might very well escalate to include yet another attempt on Sam's life.

Harley Ponyboy, Charlie Yazzie and his Uncle Thomas made up a serious set of adversaries—with the added advantage that Harley was from the area and familiar with its backcountry. But be that as it may, it still was big country. Even *they* might not be able to bring this person to ground. They might, however, be able put enough pressure on him to flush him out into the open or maybe, at least figure out who he was. The question was, would they be able to do either of these things before the man became invisible again?

Chapter 9

The Folly

Harley Ponyboy worked his ancient magic in the same methodical way he'd earned the admiration and respect of local and Federal law enforcement agencies across the Four Corners.

Fast becoming a lost art, only a handful of people on the reservation were left with the ability, and indefinable sixth sense that separates the truly exceptional tracker from the wannabe. Even as a boy, Harley had been called upon when stock went missing, or a predator wreaked havoc among area flocks. It was only natural this talent would eventually evolve to make him a tracker of men. He was from this country—attuned to its every nuance.

Harley Ponyboy knelt on one knee, studying the telltale passage of both his quarry and the tiring Sam Klah. The gritty soil, left by eons of wind and water wearing away at the towering sandstone bluffs, would make any tracker's work more difficult.

Harley picked up a cedar twig and gently touched the edge of a hoofprint, testing how it held together. Silently gauging how long since the sign was made. The clearest track was that of a horse no more than fourteen hand he decided, unshod, and typical of the old time Indian pony. The rider, heavy, and almost too much for an old pony like this, its slewing feet leaving trench-like gashes in the steeper portions of the trail. Even in that dry country the gouges had turned up a trace of moisture. Mostly evaporated now, but enough to offer a valuable timeline. *Too big a load for this little horse... already tired from the ride up here...now she's about worn out, beginning to stumble. She won't last much longer.*

Sam Klah had left a few of his own prints along the rocky trail. Clearly, he was still in hot pursuit, but in Harley's judgement gradually falling further and further behind. He knew this could change if the horse gave out, making it possible the boy might catch his assailant after all. Harley fervently hoped that wouldn't happen. This was a dangerous, well-armed assassin, who'd already made it clear the boy was his target.

Harley's mule was still fresh, compared to the laboring horse. He felt confident he was gaining, possibly within minutes now of catching up to the boy. As the trail lost altitude, the soil became finer, easier to follow.

Mounting up, Harley was able to follow the well-marked trail from the mule's back, even at a trot. The mule's natural affinity for its maternal equine-half, was zeroing in on the horse's trail. Using scent now, as much as anything else, the mule was slowly closing the gap. Harley left the pace to the animal's best judgement, thinking he might have at least one of his quarries in sight within minutes—should his calculations be right.

Topping the next small rise, the tracker spied Sam Klah almost immediately. The boy, down beside the path on his knees, cradled the old pony's head on his lap, oblivious to the approaching rider. Harley slowed the mule to a walk and advanced quietly, until he was nearly on them. The downed mare, sides heaving in the cool air, had taken notice, trying to raise her head to get up, but hadn't the strength for it.

"Did you see the man before he quit the horse?" Harley spoke in a soft voice, just loud enough to be heard over the raspy breathing of the exhausted animal. A bloody foam bubbled at the horse's nostrils, making it obvious each breath came at a cost.

The boy looked up, as though in a daze, and could only watch in silence as the man got down from his mule and moved in closer.

"No, I never saw him again after that first time this morning." Sam calmly put his hand on the old mare's neck and felt the blood pulsing through the large artery. With a helpless look at Harley Ponyboy, he finally asked, "Is there anything we can do for her?"

Harley listened again to the horse's desperate struggle to find enough air. He noted the drying lather on its flanks, and muscle tremors causing the legs to twitch. The animal, already in shock and pushed to the limit of endurance, was most likely 'wind broke'. Harley knew it unlikely this old mare would recover. Even if it did, it would never be the same. Certainly not sound enough to be ridden again.

"Give her a little longer, kid, maybe then we can get her up." Harley had seen a few horses recover from something like this, but not often, and never one this old. After watching another a moment or two, he was finally forced to admit. "She likely won't pull through this, Sam." There was no point in holding out hope to the boy when none was there. Charlie and Thomas would be along shortly. Thomas was a good tracker himself and would have little trouble following this trail—he had made certain of that.

Putting a hand on the boy's shoulder, Harley said, "Thomas and Charlie will be here soon. They know horses. We'll see what they think." Privately, he thought the horse wouldn't last that long. "I'd best get back on the trail. That yahoo's on foot now. This mule will catch up pretty quick I think." Looking up his backtrail, Harley knew the others would be along any minute. "They will bring along a spare horse for you and, if they think you are up to coming along, you can still get in on this. I'm certain this bastard's not far now." With that, Harley swung back up on the mule and turned down the trail. He knew he would have to catch this man unaware, and within revolver range—should it come to that.

~~~~~

Thomas, well in the lead of Charlie's gelding, was bent low in the saddle, reading Harley Ponyboy's sign, raising his head from time to time to make sure Charlie was keeping up. When at last they came into sight, he could see that, both the Tribal Investigator and his horse, needed a moment to catch their breath. Keeping the pack mule and spare saddle horse moving had held Charlie back. He rarely found time to ride horseback these days and those muscles peculiar to covering rough country horseback, were now signaling they'd had enough and needed a rest. A fast, downhill pace is most always tough on man and horse, and this trail had been falling off toward the low country at an alarming rate, almost since they'd started out.

Apologizing, between gulps of the cold canyon air, Charlie said, "I had to get off back there and walk a bit to limber up, shake the kinks out."

"Charlie-horses, huh?" Thomas smiled.

"Something like that, I guess." Charlie grinned sheepishly, obviously embarrassed by his lack of condition. He hadn't realized how out of shape he was, until now. Dragging the mule and spare horse along behind him through several thick patches, had taken it out of him.

"Well, I can understand how being a desk jockey is a lot tougher than chasing bad guys cross-country horseback. Maybe you should get out more."

The Legal Services Investigator nodded again as he caught his breath. "I know. Even my horse is out of shape."

Concentrating on the more obvious sign Harley had left behind, Thomas kept his own horse to a quick and steady pace. This, despite the added chore of puzzling out several different sets of comingled tracks. The lanky Navajo frowned at his friend and ventured a forgone opinion, "This man we're following seems to know the country pretty well. He's good at finding the quickest way down. Looks like Harley's staying with him so far though. Still, I can't help thinking this bastard might have a few more tricks up his sleeve."

Charlie nodded as he tugged at the mule's lead rope, looking cautiously past Thomas to the plunging way ahead, he held his horse back. At this point, the spare saddle horse was pretty much on its own. It had pulled loose some time back up the trail, but being well broke to the work, still managed to find the occasional opportunity to nip at the recalcitrant mule's behind, urging him along and letting him know who was boss.

Thomas kept an eye on his slower friend and, watching as the pack mule began to fret and stomp his feet, was fearful the loose horse might decide to quit the country altogether. Calling back to him he said, "What you might ought to have done is lead that horse we brought for Sam and turn the mule loose. He would have kept up better following your horse rather than looking back to keep track of it."

Charlie, knowing this was probably true, but not having time to make up an excuse, chose to ignore thejibe. "I just hope our friend's not forgetting this guy has a rifle and might lay for him if pressed too hard."

"That's exactly what I was thinking." Thomas swung off his horse and tightened the cinch another notch before it could take a deep breath. "You'd think Harley would know that though, should he even be taking time to think." He looked down the trail as though seeing something no one else could. "Surely he's come up on the boy by now. I would imagine that head wound has to be holding the kid back some. To be honest, I'm surprised he's made it this far. I guess he might be a little tougher than I thought."

Charlie smiled inwardly at this. Thomas was coming around. *Still a long way from giving away his daughter, but it's a start.* In his own heart, the Investigator held little hope for this young couple ever getting together. For the young, however, he knew hope was a more durable commodity than for the rest of us. He sighed at these passing thoughts of youth and, with a slight shake of his head, he got down to tighten his own horse's cinch.

~~~~~~

Thomas Begay was bent on working sign and wasn't watching ahead as closely as he might have been. From his place behind, and a little higher on the trail it was Charlie Yazzie who was first to spot the boy and whistle ahead to alert Thomas.

Glancing back to see Charlie urging him forward, he kicked his horse into a trot, despite the treacherous way down.

Jerking on the pack mule's lead rope, Charlie followed as fast as his prudent nature would allow. The spare saddle horse, finally putting aside its last vestige of patience, careened past both mule and man to join the leaders down the trail.

Thomas Begay, outdistancing his slower friend by a good bit, finally spotted the boy as he sat beside his downed horse. Slowing his mount to a walk, he approached the miserable looking Sam Klah, who looked up briefly and then leaned back against a tree. He gave little notice he was even aware of Thomas. The older man pulled up his horse as the boy continued gazing silently at his old mare, now lying still beside the trail. The mare must have been the last vestige of his old life and he was having a hard time letting her go.

Climbing down, Thomas glanced at the horse and then at the boy. "Dead?"

The boy nodded slowly, not answering the man's questioning gaze.

Thomas took in the dirty bandage on the boy's wound. "How's the head?"

The boy looked up, involuntarily touching a hand to his forehead as he rose unsteadily to his feet, all the while holding to the tree for support.

Thomas moved to the horse, nudging it with the toe of his boot. "Well, that's a Damn shame. It's a sorry man who punishes a horse like this. I expect the Sonofabitch will pay for it, in this life or the other. I'd like to think so, anyway."

Thomas turned to the boy and quickly reached out a hand as he saw him take a deep breath and start to sag. Putting a hand on the boy's shoulder, he eased Sam back down beside the tree. "We'll have to get a fresh bandage on that head. It's full of dirt and starting to bleed again." He looked up the backtrail. "Charlie's right behind me with a pack mule, He'll likely fix that right up."

Sam Klah touched the bandage again, but easier this time, releasing his breath in a jerky sigh as he tried to blink away the ache in his head. "I'll be alright, I just need a few minutes, he said"

"When did you eat last?"

"This morning, I guess, but I'm not really hungry. I'd rather get back after that man before he gets away."

"Harley won't let him get away." He wished he was as sure of that as he made it sound. For Harley's sake he almost wished this outlaw *would* get away, rather than see his old friend's life at risk. He had every confidence in Harley's ability to even the odds posed by the man's rifle, but even so, he couldn't help thinking, *The Sonofabitch could still get lucky.*

Chapter 10

The Escape

Late that evening, Billy Red Clay found the three men and the boy Sam Klah, sitting around the dying embers of a fire, coffee pot still simmering in the coals. Their camp by the creek, now missing all but one tent, was looking almost abandoned, and a gloomier gathering he had seldom witnessed. Harley Ponyboy, with a bandaged left foot, now carefully elevated by a chunk of firewood, eyed his own injury with disgust.

The boy's head, though freshly bandaged, was already showing seepage. Every one of them appeared worn out and seriously disappointed in their failure to catch the murderous cutthroat. Each man knew it was likely he would continue to target the boy, for what reason, they couldn't imagine.

The Navajo Policeman came past the horse trailers with little more than a glance, but it was enough to tell him the animals were equally jaded, heads down, eyes nearly closed and barely picking at their feed. The mules wore the signatory lop-eared badge of defeat common among their tribe.

Billy edged into the circle around the fire and sat himself down amongst them without speaking, taking pains not to look directly at anyone. After a long silence his Uncle Thomas handed him his empty cup and indicated the coffee pot with a push of his chin. Billy filled the cup and set back to wait. No one appeared interested in offering up an explanation for what must have been a significant rout—one striking to the core of their manly pride.

There was no sign of food having been prepared and that alone spoke to the depth of their despair. Billy could see he would have to initiate a conversation if one was to be had, knowing even this breach of etiquette might prove unproductive.

The Policeman sat back and sipped his coffee, spitting the stirred-up grounds into the embers as he worked down to the dregs. Finally, indicating Harley Ponyboy's bandaged foot with raised eyebrows, he took the plunge. "Did you get shot, Harley?"

The afflicted man shook his head, no, but didn't offer up any further explanation of the injury.

Looking cautiously around the circle Billy tried again. "So, no one got shot?" After a few more moments of silence, the Policeman was forced to take this for a 'no' and muttered under his breath, "Well I guess that's a good thing." *At least the day wasn't a total disaster.* Smiling to himself he tossed the empty cup back toward his Uncle who automatically snatched it out of the air and fixed his Nephew with a contemplative air, one implying disapproval.

Billy had grown up around these men and didn't care to rile them should they not be of a mind to talk. They would eventually, of course, if he didn't push the issue. It was the Navajo way to avoid an unpleasantness as long as possible, thinking perhaps it might go away on its own if it were ignored long enough.

He studied Charlie Yazzie across the smoldering firepit. A *modern, educated Navajo* he was thinking. A person he respected and one he'd made considerable effort to emulate, he'd expected more from Charlie Yazzie. He should have known the man would feel it best to let the others tell their own story. The other two were traditionalists for the most part, and Billy Red Clay could understand this. He was inclined to cut them some slack. After waiting another few minutes, however, his patience began to wear thin, causing him to look askance at each in turn. *Dammit, I'm an Officer of the law. It's my job to get to the bottom of things.* Clearing his throat, and taking in enough air to last him, Billy made his move.

"So, Uncle," he said softly, "Lucy told me in town someone took a shot at you people and you went after them." He looked Thomas directly in the eye knowing this was a thing his Uncle would take as an affront he couldn't ignore. "Did the guy get away, or what?"

Thomas Begay didn't hesitate to answer this time, addressing the question with a curt reply. "Yes, he did, Nephew. Harley here, jumped him out of the brush without the man getting off a shot." He let this hang in the air for a moment before saying with a sigh, "Then Harley broke his damned ankle on a rock hopping off his mule."

Harley Ponyboy then felt obligated to speak up and launched into his side of the story without denying any part of Thomas's statement. "I was flat on my back, but I already had my revolver out and was able to get off a quick shot at the man, that's probably what saved my life. I don't think I hit him, but it let him know I wasn't defenseless, and could still do him some harm. Or, it may have been that he heard Thomas's horse pounding down the trail and wondered how many more were coming for him. Maybe he figured the odds weren't in his favor and just...dropped back in the brush and disappeared."

Thomas angrily interrupted. "He's a murdering coward who kills from hiding...or tries to. When I rode in on them, I saw Harley laying on the ground, thinking he'd been shot, I pulled up to see to him first." He slung his head in frustration. "When I found Harley wasn't in any immediate danger of dying, I went after the man on foot. There was no way I could get a horse in there, but by then he'd disappeared. I tried to find his trail but couldn't. Harley is the only one that might have tracked him in such cover as that, and it might have been iffy even for him. Whoever it is knows his way around out here. I doubt we'll get up on him again anytime soon. But there's no guarantee he won't try to get up on us."

Billy Red Clay turned next to Sam Klah. "Sam, do you have any idea who might want to kill you, or even why?" He stared the boy down and went on. "This is the second time someone has made an attempt on your life in as many days. The first time could have been laid to a random act of horse-thievery or whatever, but from what I understand, this last incident was, without a doubt, a planned effort to kill you. There has to be a reason for something like this, and we need to get to the bottom of that before he tries again. And I might add, we'll be dammed lucky to get a second chance at him.

What can you tell us about all this? Is there anyone you can think of who might have reason to want you dead?"

After a moment of silence on the boy's part, Charlie, who was sitting alongside, gently nudged him whispering something no one else could hear.

Sam Klah sat up straight and, taking a deep breath, said in a clear voice, "I am nobody, and I've never hurt nobody. I don't have any idea who might have it in for me like this. Maybe someone put a curse on me for some reason."

Charlie Yazzie had been expecting something like this and, rolling his eyes, looked across at the Tribal Policeman, both nodding as though familiar with this reasoning.

Thomas and Harley looked down, suddenly not sure themselves that some sort of witchery wasn't at the root of the thing. Thomas Begay, especially, found the idea intriguing, nodding wisely at his friend Harley to show his silent support.

Looking over at the two law men, and finding no encouragement from that quarter, Thomas jumped up and declared "I'm hungry. Let's make us something to eat." And, so saying, went to the coolers to take stock of what their wives might have left them. Quickly joining in the effort, Sam Klah began carrying firewood from the other, recently abandoned campsites, then set to building up the fire and helping Thomas with the food.

Charlie motioned to Billy Red Clay, and the pair left to take the still-dehydrated stock to the creek for a last drink of water. Tribal Investigator Yazzie, anxious to hear what Billy had learned that morning in town, made it clear from the start he was aware some of it might be privileged information, not for everyone's ears.

As soon as they were out of earshot, Billy exclaimed, "You are not going to believe what Fred Smith turned up on Erwin Johnson."

"What?"

"Well, back in the day, he worked at Legal Services!"

Charlie stopped midstride, turned to the Tribal Cop with doubt clearly written on every feature. "Billy are you sure?"

"No, but Agent Smith is. Says he has a folder full of evidence to back it up."

"Well, I'll just be damned," Charlie still couldn't believe it and was still shaking his head at the notion when he declared, "Surely, I'd have heard something about that? I've been there a lot of years now." The Tribal Investigator grew quiet for a moment, then said, "I did think his name sounded a little familiar when it came through on your report, but thought I might have seen it in one of our case files or something. What was this guy's job supposed to be?"

"Fred just said he was a higher up. He was Office Manager, briefly, and then head of a special section, had a couple of accountants working under him—mostly involved in the uranium lawsuits back then. I didn't know this last part until Fred called me on the radio on my way out here. Even after interviewing the man, I was as much surprised to hear all this as you are." He looked over at Charlie. "Fred mentioned *you* might know someone in the office you could wheedle something out of."

As they were finishing up with the animals, Charlie preoccupied, had to retie a mule to the picket line a second time. *Pete Fish was Office manager when I came on board, I don't think I ever heard who was in charge before that.* Pulling himself out of the past, he admitted. "There *is* an old fellow from back then. I believe I heard he once worked in records, and about that same time period, too. Nice enough old man from what I've seen of him. He works case files now. As I remember it, he came up for retirement some years back, but chose to stay on. Couldn't afford to quit, he said."

"Are you going back in tomorrow?" Billy was seeing a glimmer of hope now and thought it urgent Charlie should pursue this lead as soon as possible, slim though the possibilities might be.

"I think we're all heading back to town in the morning, Billy. When I get back in the office, I'll get up with the old man and see what he has to say about Erwin Johnson."

"Good! Oh, and before I forget it, I also had the Bureau check into Sam's Uncle."

"Sam will be happy to hear that. What turned up on him? Anything that might help the boy locate him?"

"No, much as I hate to tell you, they couldn't. In Fred's words, 'We couldn't find a Damn thing on the man, nothing, zilch, zero." Billy reflected on this a moment. "That's kind of funny, don't you think? It was a first for me. The FBI unable to place someone on the Reservation? They have access to almost everything the BIA has, in addition to their own files—not to mention Tribal Agency files, yet nothing comes up anywhere." The Navajo Cop snorted as he slapped his gloves at a mosquito.

"That doesn't make any sense—does it, Billy?"

"No, it doesn't but like Fred says, there's more than one person out here who's running under the radar. I know that to be true from my own experience, and so do you."

Charlie looked away with a grimace, indicating a grudging show of agreement. His mood brightened, however, when he thought of his last conversation with Professor Custer. "You know, Billy, Sam may not even need to fall back on his Uncle."

"Oh, how so?"

"Doc Custer has agreed to take Sam in to help him in his work. Says he seems like a nice enough boy and has an obvious inclination for learning. I think it could be a good thing for both of them. George has plenty of room there at his place in Farmington and says Sam can stay right there with him for the time being."

Billy mulled this over. "Probably for the best. It's beginning to look like Sam's Uncle may not be the most upright person to take him in. I'm not sure why I say that, but for a gut feeling I had from something Erwin Johnson said. Things appear to be a little sketchy with this Uncle of his. We've been able to find out basically nothing about him, and that in itself tells us something."

"Well, let's leave it at that then. I'll drop Sam off at the Doc's place in the morning and well go from there." Privately, Charlie was convinced this might be a real opportunity for the boy—should he apply himself. Professor Custer had been a teacher for the better part of his life and knew the Navajo way of thinking better than most white people. *Yes, this might be the very thing for both of them.* Charlie, satisfied with this thinking, looked skyward. "Nice night. There's going to be a big moon too, the kids would have enjoyed seeing it. I'm sure Harley would have had a big story to go along with it."

Back at the fire, the others were standing expectantly, holding bowls and spoons, and watching Thomas Begay tend a large pot of something bubbling over the coals. Harley was tottering around on one foot, with a hand on Sam Klah's shoulder to keep his balance. Sam, himself, was not all that steady on his feet, and Charlie called over to the pair.

"We can bring you two your supper, you know, you could have stayed seated."

Thomas shrugged. "I already told 'em that." Giving the pair a toss of his head, he said, "By the time you two get over here there may not be any left anyway."

Harley was the one who spoke up. "We needed to get up and move around a little anyway. Besides I'd like to see what's in that pot for myself, Thomas isn't exactly known for his *gourmet* cooking."

Charlie looked up at the man's use of the word and smiled.

Thomas turned, holding up a ladle. "I'm surprised you even know the meaning of the word, Harley. You're coming right along. Money might not make the man, but it hasn't hurt the Harley." For some reason Thomas found this humorous beyond all reckoning and was still chuckling when he started serving up the stew—if that was what it was.

Chapter 11

The Calling

Ida Marie Begay sat slumped at the kitchen table. Old man Paul T'Sosi, sitting directly across from the girl, had already noticed her being out of sorts this morning. Having heard the story of the family camping trip and its abrupt end, the old man concluded, her mood had something to do with the boy at the center of the incident.

"Granddaughter, tell me again about that boy you brought back to life."

The girl gave a roll of her eyes as she considered her Grandfather. Paul wasn't really her grandfather at all, yet both she and her brother had long considered him as such, and gratefully so. He was the only grandfather they'd known, and they'd thought a great deal of him from the start. As she watched from the corner of an eye, she couldn't help thinking how much older he looked of late, more so than she'd ever seen him. More wrinkles, and more gray hair than she remembered, too. Paul seemed somehow to have grown smaller in the last year. It was as though he was fading away before her eyes.

"Grandfather! I already told you—I didn't save Sam's life. It wasn't like that at all. I just helped take care of him when he got hurt." This came out sharper than she meant it, but the old man seemed not to notice.

With a twinkle in his eye, he persisted. "You said he wants to get married with you didn't you? That's what I heard. What about that?"

Ida Marie turned to peer out the kitchen window. She could see the rest of the family down at the corrals tending to the sheep, and her brother Caleb tossing a little hay to the horses. She should have been down there with them. But she, being a late riser, had this morning been charged with fixing her grandfather's breakfast when he showed up for his morning coffee.

Paul T'Sosi had long refused to live in the big house, though he still took his meals there and made a point of dropping by a few times a day for coffee—mainly just to see what was going on—and see what sort of advice he might offer. For the most part, however, he said he preferred his old *hogan*. Being only steps away allowed him to keep his eye on the family, which he still considered his duty. Thomas had built this new house for his wife and children, but added an extra bedroom for his father-in-law, thinking it would bring he and the old man closer together. They had never gotten along all that well, not from the very beginning. When Paul did finally begin getting along with his son-in-law, well, that's when people finally realized Paul was getting old.

The old Singer maintained the new place had no memories—no soul. "Fine enough for young people," he would say. "They have time enough to make their own memories. But for someone like me, and close to the end of the Beauty Path, I need a little more peace and quiet to study on what might be coming next."

Ida Marie, taking her que from Lucy Tallwoman, didn't like it when Paul talked like this. Like her stepmother, she would change the subject or ignore the old man's remarks entirely. Of late, however, Paul's mind had begun to wander more frequently—his thoughts sometimes harder to decipher. Ida Marie sometimes had to remind herself of who he was, and the respect that was owed him by the entire family.

Turning herself back to their current conversation, Ida spoke more carefully. "It is just that... this family doesn't take Sam Klah seriously. They think he's just some country boy who doesn't know what he's talking about, doesn't realize how things are done in today's world. I can't make them understand, he's not like that at all. He's intelligent, and constantly thinking how he can earn a place for himself, if people would just give him a chance."

Paul listened to this, nodding in his chair, giving every indication he was on the verge of dozing off, but when the girl leaned closer to see if this was the case, the old man opened one eye and asked, "Is he good looking? That would just about make him perfect, I would think."

Ida Marie grimaced at this... "Well, I think so."

Paul began talking then, quietly at first but becoming stronger as he went on. "Don't think, Granddaughter, that I do not understand. It has been a long time, but I remember how it was to be young." He tapped the table with a bony forefinger. "It will take a while for some people to get used to this boy, and it won't happen overnight, either! That's how it was with your father, when he came here, but I finally got used to him, more or less. Not everyone will come around to this way of thinking at the same time. It will probably be easier for some of us, than for others, but it will come, have no doubt of that. The boy has tradition on his side for one thing." Then, pausing to reflect a moment, he said, "being good looking doesn't hurt though."

The girl glanced at the old man taking her time before answering, "I hope you are right Grandfather, because he is not going to give up, and neither will I."

Paul smiled at this. "I have no doubt in my mind about that, Ida. I will bring this up with Thomas and my daughter. I imagine they think you are just too young and haven't given this enough thought. They may have forgotten how they were when they were your age. I'll remind them." The old man had a faraway look in his eye when he said, "By and by, the world will come right for you—you'll see." Then a frown fell across Paul's face. "Where is this boy now? I would like to see this Sam Klah for myself."

The girl, looking down at her lap, shook her head. "No one will tell me where he is. they say no one should know until he's out of danger. They said that person from the canyons could still be looking for him." Ida Marie had to stop and think about this next thing before saying it. "My mother, did let it slip she thinks Charlie Yazzie knows."

The old man chuckled, "Do you remember when you were a little girl and Charlie and your Father rescued you from that Ute camp up on the Uinta?"

Ida smiled, despite herself. "I remember alright. How could anyone forget something like that?" Ida Marie reached across the table and touched her

Grandfather's hand. "It was pretty exciting stuff for a young girl, getting snatched up and made off with by a father she hardly even knew, then being chased by a bunch of Ute women screaming bloody murder. I'll never forget that."

"I hope you don't forget it, Granddaughter, and you should never forget what it tells you: how much your father loved you even then, that he would risk his life to come for you. And don't forget Charlie Yazzie, either. Thomas would never have found you without Charlie's help. That's why your father says Charlie is your Uncle. He says Charlie earned it." The old man chuckled silently as he recalled the story, and how Charlie had previously rescued the girl's brother from the Utes as well. Nearly got shot for his trouble then, too. "Every one of us has your happiness and best interest at heart, I hope you'll keep that in *your* heart. Please, Granddaughter, try to have a little more patience with us." Then the old man smiled a little and looked down at the table. "Thomas can be stubborn, no one knows that better than me, and yet now, here we are getting along like crows and magpies."

Ida Marie picked up her head with a scowl. "Crows and magpies don't get along all that well, I don't think."

The old man sighed, "I know."

Pulling out of the Farmington Mall, Harley Sr. shook a finger at his son sitting beside him, a dark cloud beginning to settle across his brow. The three-year-old wanted a new pair of boots this morning, but this was where his father drew the line. "You have two pair of boots at home now that are still like new, you'll likely outgrow those before you get much wear out of them."

Harley Ponyboy was learning about being a parent, but it had been slow going. He still didn't have a perfect understanding of how a child's mind works, and at this point, wasn't sure anyone else did either.

"When I was your age, I only had one pair of pants and one shirt to my name—and they were so worn out it's a wonder I wasn't arrested for indecent exposure."

Little Harley sat listening to his father. He'd heard it all before. He didn't understand it, but it was imprinted on his memory. Someday he would look back on these things and smile, knowing at last what his father had meant, and what message was intended. Occasionally the boy would look down at the stack of new clothes in his lap with a more tolerant look, a look his father wasn't allowed to see. Sue Yazzie always said he had his father 'wrapped.' He didn't know exactly what that meant but had learned the hard way that she was seldom wrong.

Harley Ponyboy wasn't through yet, and continued with a new vigor, "So, don't be whining about the color of that shirt. The lady said it was mauve." And thought to himself *this must be a new name for purple.* "And it was the last one they had in your size. So quit bellyaching, Junior."

"Don' call me 'Junior'! I don' like dat name."

Harley smirked at this. "Well, you better get used to it, you're going to hear it a lot on down the line."

The boy scowled, "Where we going? I wanna' go home. My cartoons comin' on in jus' a minute."

"No, Harley, they *aren't* coming on in jus a minute. We'll be home in plenty of time for those cartoons."

The little boy mumbled something Harley couldn't hear and frowned fiercely out the window.

"Since we are going right past the Doc's place, I thought we'd drop by and maybe have a little visit with him. You like George, and he likes you, too. Maybe he'll give you a sucker if he still has any left in his desk drawer. Although you did hit his supply pretty hard last time we were here."

The boy brightened considerably at the prospect of seeing 'Doc', as he called him. He put on a different face entirely, smiling up at his father in a show of reconciliation, thinking to himself; *I got Doc wrapped, too.*

Harley knew his son was spoiled, but most Navajo tend to indulge their children to one extent or another, and they might be considered spoiled in an outsider's view. Harley, however, had not yet snapped to the notion that he was the one causing it. The fact of the business was little Harley was only doing what any other child would do under the same circumstances. It was just human nature at work, that's what it was.

Pulling up to the Professor's office, Harley cautioned his son a final time regarding his manners. "Don't be asking Doc for a sucker as soon as you hit the door. If he has any left, he'll offer you one without you asking."

The little boy, tongue in cheek in anticipation, gave a solemn nod of his head but a tiny smile was on his lips. He was ready.

It was Professor George Armstrong Custer himself that answered the knock. Harley pushed his son to the fore as George smiled, first at the father, and then down at the boy. "Well now, who have we here?"

Thinking George might have forgotten who they were, the boy piped up, "I'm Harley. We are bof' Harleys, Doc."

"So you are, little man, so you are." Ushering the pair into the house, the Professor patted the boy on the head. "What brings you gentlemen into town today?"

"Oh, we was just in the neighborhood and thought we would drop by for a little visit, if you are not too busy."

George chuckled, "I always have time for you Harleys."

Harley Jr. then tugged at the Professor's pant leg. "I wanna' sucka' Doc."

Harley thumped the boy on the head with a forefinger. "What did I just tell you in the truck? If George has a sucker, he'll offer you one when he's good and ready. You don't go around begging for suckers, it's not polite."

George held up a hand. "Boys, if all it's going to take to settle this is a sucker, I believe I might just have one left." The Professor went to his desk across the room and, sifting through a drawer, came up with the treat he held up for the boy to see. "Aha!" he said holding the candy out to little Harley. "Here you are little man."

The boy glanced up at his father with a triumphant grin. "See! If you wanna' sucka' you gotta ast for a sucka." Running over to Professor Custer the little boy hugged him as he took the prize.

George smiled down at the boy. "Eat that later, in your father's new truck, Harley. I don't want to be sticking to everything in the house."

Stuffing the candy in his pocket the boy agreed without a whimper.

Harley Ponyboy was giving his son the look, as he and Doc seated themselves at the table. The Professor's house was not furnished in any conventional sort of way, doubling as it did, as both his home and place of business. The living room walls were temporarily lined with shelving holding at least a part of the yield from his recent dig. Harley Jr. was immediately attracted to the artifacts and, not surprisingly, paid little attention to his father's warnings.

"Look but don't touch, Harley!" Then, lowering his voice, but still with an eye on his son, asked, "So, how is Sam, Doc?"

"I figured Charlie would tell you and Thomas where he was, but we did agree no one else was to know."

"That's what he said to me all right. I'm not supposed to know."

"Sam's out back, in the shed, sorting through some of the things we recovered from Spring Canyon and hopefully cataloging some of the stuff we brought back this last run." He paused and smiled at his longtime friend. "That was one of the jobs you used to have, if you'll remember." When he went on, his voice grew more serious. "No one that I know of has any inkling who this young man is, or what he's doing here. He's a good boy, Harley, and will make a good man, should he keep his head about him. He's a hard worker, and easy to get along with. I'm not able to pay him much, but he seems satisfied for the time being. He's a big help around here, and I would be inclined to keep him on, but with this current dig finishing up, I'm not sure how much I would have for him to do. I suspect he has other plans in mind, especially where Ida Begay is concerned. I've done my best to convince him they should wait a couple of years on the marriage thing, but can't say how much of that stuck, if any. In my opinion, there's not much to be done about it at this point. Kids these days seem to do what they will, no matter what."

"What's Charlie thinking, or has he even said?"

"I don't believe he's got that far yet. He did say he thinks the boy might be better off here right now, than any place else he can think of."

Harley mulled this over. "Well, you know there *is* one other place, and I'm kinda' surprised you didn't think of it."

"Oh, and where would that be?"

Harley smiled. "Aida Winter's place, north of Cortez."

George looked stunned for a moment, finally saying, "You might be right, Harley. Aida's someone who would likely want to help with something like this." The Professor appeared to become more pleased with the idea the longer he thought of it. "The woman could use some help up there and can well afford to pay him what he's worth, something I can't do just now. The last time I talked with Aida, she told me she's had to cut back on her horse operation because she can't keep up with it anymore." The Professor beamed. "You may be on to something here Harley. Maybe you could ask Charlie what he thinks when he gets home this evening. I know I'd be happy to put in a word for the boy, and I'm sure Charlie would vouch for him as well. Not wishing Sam and Ida any bad luck, but a little more separation between them might not be such a bad thing right now."

"Speaking of Aida, George, I've been meaning to ask, have you been up to see her lately? There's a lot of history between you two. Just wondering how you and her were getting along these days?"

"Oh, we get along fine. We just don't see each other as often as we used to, not that I wouldn't like to, but we are both pretty busy these days and haven't had a chance to get together as much as we once did. And to be honest, I'm not sure she's past all that."

Harley nodded sadly at this. "Well, that's too bad Doc. I always thought the two of you were good for each other, but then, what the hell do I know about that stuff anyway?" Then, as though another thought had occurred to him, "You know Doc, Ida Marie and her brother Caleb spend a few weeks each year up there with Aida, toward the end of summer, and have done so since they were little." Harley had a quizzical look on his face when he whispered, "How do you think that might work out, with Sam being there? If that should even happen."

Custer smiled. "Summer's a long way off, Harley. The situation might well resolve itself before then. Keep in mind, Sam and Ida will both be eighteen soon. It will be up to them what happens after that. If this is meant to be, a short separation won't deter them."

Chapter 12

The Consideration

Charlie Yazzie pulled up to his mailbox and was already rolling down his window when he noticed Harley Ponyboy and his son coming down their fork of the drive. The mailman was new to the job and, with this larger route, generally came later in the day. Little Harley was in tow, laughing as his father lifted him by the hand and swung him across a puddle. Retrieving his mail, Charlie backed his truck up to allow his neighbors access to their mailbox.

He paused to study the pair, amused to see them, once again, dressed exactly alike—right down to the bright red kerchiefs, tucked in the collar of their new denim shirts. Harley seemed to think dressing alike somehow identified them as father and son, though anyone with half an eye would say their looks and facial expressions alone left little doubt of their relationship.

Waving a greeting, big Harley stopped at his mailbox and opened it, only to jump back, flinging the boy behind him. "Sonofa..."

Charlie, surprised, saw something fall, writhing in the air even as it hit the ground. Rattlesnake! He could hear the whir of its rattles as it coiled, striking short as Harley kicked at it with a booted foot, retreating farther back as he shielded his son.

Charlie jumped out of the truck and grabbed the first thing to hand, a garden hoe he'd left in the pickup's bed the day before. He caught the snake with a vicious chop behind the head, separating it from the still writhing body. In all their years there, he had never seen a rattler anywhere near the property.

Harley picked up his son and moved a little closer, that the boy might see the still moving creature. Little Harley, frightened by the snake's headless death throes, clung more tightly to his father. The elder Harley's traditional upbringing might have prevented him from killing the creature himself and later admitted he likely would have just let it go.

Charlie, on the other hand, felt no such qualms. Acting on the spur of the moment, he was more intent on safeguarding his children, whose bus stop was only steps away.

Charlie threw down the hoe in disgust. "Harley, someone put that snake there for a reason. The question is, was it a random act of mischief, or was it meant for you specifically?"

"Well, if it were deliberate, it had to have something to do with this guy we was tracking. Then, too, it may have been meant as warning of some sort."

"Maybe." Charlie wasn't so sure. It had taken some planning, and considerable knowhow. *You don't just go out and pick up a rattlesnake this time of year. Most are starting to den-up by now.* He was sure Harley knew this, but figured the man was having a hard time accepting the fact that someone might do such a thing. "There's one thing for certain, Harley, whoever did this didn't care who got hurt. Not many people think like that."

Harley had set his son down and the boy was now at the side of the road, peering into the brush where the snake was still writhing.

"I guess you may be right. My son, or any other little kid, could have been the one to open that mailbox." A strange look was on his face as he stepped over and picked up his Harley. Hugging the boy tighter, he turned back to the Investigator. "How would they know my name, or where I live?"

This stumped his friend. For once, Charlie had no answer. "I don't know, Harley. I just don't know." He got back in the truck and flung open the passenger side door. "Get in. I'll give you two a ride up to the house."

Harley Ponyboy, still clutching his son, nodded. "Okay. There was another thing I was wanting ta talk about, anyhow." Settling into the seat, with Harley Jr. on his lap, he launched into the high points of his visit to Professor Custer's that morning. After a personal assessment of how things were going at the Professor's, he fixed Charlie with a contemplative eye. "Me and the Doc was talking about Sam Klah, and he thinks he might run out of work for him before long, at least until he can scare up another contract. We were thinking a safer place might be up to Aida Winter's place. The Doc says she could use some help up there, and he trusts her to keep it to herself. She's not a big talker anyway, as you know." Harley gave his still worried son a squeeze. "The pay would likely be good, too. Something to think about, Charlie."

Charlie ran this around in his mind a time or two before nodding cautiously in agreement, deciding it might, in fact, be the best thing for Sam after all. The Investigator then filled Harley in on Fred Smith's report on both Erwin Johnson, and Sam Klah's Uncle, John Etcitty. "Someone's out to get that boy, and while it might not be either one of these two, we can't rule them out at this point, either."

Harley sighed and looked down at his son. "Well, there's no doubt in my mind, someone deliberately put that rattler in my mailbox, as a warning maybe, but it could have turned out deadly serious for me or my son."

Charlie stared at his friend a moment. "That's why I decided your personal stake in this thing is deserving of whatever information comes my way. I intend you to be kept in the loop from now on." He looked toward his own house at the end of the lane. "From here on in, Sue and I will be keeping a closer eye on your place. She said you can drop the boy off with her anytime you need to."

Harley nodded his thanks, then shrugged. "I expect whoever put that snake in there, did it after dark last night. It was probably starting to get hot this afternoon, that's what got him riled up. Probably why he struck the way he did."

Charlie knew his friend was feeling some guilt over the snake being killed, so was he, but to a much lesser degree. "Old Man Paul would likely do a cleansing for you, Harley, he's not very busy these days."

Harley nodded, scratching his jaw in thought. "Oh, I'm sure he would do it, but it wouldn't do any good just now, I'd just have to have him do another one, later on—after I kill this son-of-a-bitch."

"Harley, you know this kind of thinking's not good for your *Hozo*, and that means it's not good for you or your son."

"No, maybe it isn't, but I'm starting to realize that person up in the canyons isn't someone the law is likely to catch. This isn't just about Sam Klah anymore—it's about me and my boy now, too. No, I think it's time I took a bigger hand in this myself, if I ever want it over and done with."

Charlie realized he'd been holding his breath and let it out with a deep sigh, thinking *this is not the time to try talking Harley Ponyboy out of anything.*

~~~~~

When Charlie arrived at the office the next morning his first thought was to see if Norman Klee, down in records, had come in. He'd asked about the old man the day before, only to be told he worked only four days a week and that day wasn't one of them.

This morning, however, the head of Legal Services found his receptionist ready for him. Arlene turned as he came in the door and bobbed her head in his direction.

Having anticipated his question, she spoke first. "He's here alright, just came in a few minutes ago...early as usual. I didn't say a word about any of this to him." She lowered an eyelid, "He's a nice old guy, Mr. Yazzie; try to go easy on him. He's an old man and not in very good health."

Charlie stared at the woman a moment. "I wasn't planning on tar and feathering him, Arlene, just a few questions about something, something that happened a long time ago That's all. Nothing to be concerned about."

She nodded. "That's good, Boss, I could ask him those questions for you, if you like?"

"No, Arlene, that's quite all right." Charlie winked conspiratorially. "Oh, and thanks for having records pull his file. Could you bring that back to the office for me later, please?"

"It's already on your desk, Chief, I put it there first thing."

Back in his office the Investigator immediately began going through Norman Klee's file. It didn't take long. Charlie thought the report a little light considering the length of time the man had worked there, a surprising amount of time, in fact. Mr. Klee was someone who'd kept a low profile over the years. A good worker, who showed up when he was supposed to and never caused any trouble, even when passed over for advancement, which had apparently occurred more than once. Charlie could remember seeing the man coming and going, from time to time, but never seemed able to remember what his job was. He knew only that Norman Klee worked in the downstairs offices, a place he seldom had occasion to visit. Now that he was head of Legal, however, that would have to change. He picked up the receiver and keyed Arlene's line. "Arlene, should Mr. Klee not be tied up at the moment, could you please have him come up here to my office?"

"Right away, Chief." Arlene had a habit of starting off the morning addressing him as Mr. Yazzie, but as the day wore on, gravitated to Boss, then eventually, Chief, which he often thought was said tongue-in-cheek. Most people thought the woman a little odd, but she was a good receptionist who knew what was going on and kept it to herself. That, and being there longer than most, made her the exception to a long and temporary string of nonperformers.

Through the windowed door to the outer office, Charlie kept an eye on the desks as they began filling up, glancing at the clock only once or twice before spotting Norman Klee, shuffling through the loose scatter of workstations. Seeing the old man hesitate at the door, he rose to meet him and quickly moved to invite him in.

"Ah, Mr. Klee, come in, come in and have a seat. I'll try not to take too long this morning."

Charlie pointed to the chair across the desk from his own and again motioned him to have a seat. As the old man settled himself, the Investigator studied him a moment before sitting back down. He was surprised how old he looked, and frail to the point Charlie felt guilty he hadn't gone down to see *him* rather than causing the man to come upstairs. He extended a hand across the desk, rising halfway to shake hands. Finding the man's grip surprisingly strong Charlie thought perhaps he may have underestimated the old fellow's health.

"Norman, as I'm sure you know, I haven't been in this position very long and I'm afraid I've been a bit lax in getting around to introducing myself to everyone in our downstairs offices. How's everything going for you down there?"

The old man, after thinking it over a moment, slowly nodded his head as an indicator that things were going along all right.

Seeing the man glance over at the open file on his desk Charlie could see Norman was already aware the papers had been requested in advance. "Sorry I missed you yesterday Norman. I wasn't aware it was your day off." He tapped the file folder with a forefinger. "You, sir, have a long and admirable history here at Legal

Services, one to be proud of I might add. Not everyone here can say as much."

The old man, staring at the folder, said, almost as though to himself, "I've never seen that file." Then, taking a deep breath, he admitted, "Even though I oversee much of what goes on down there these days, it has long been the rule that employees do not have access to their own files."

Charlie nodded, impressed by the man's frankness. Still, he couldn't help thinking, *it's hard to believe a person wouldn't occasionally take a peek at his own file.* "You were once the section manager, were you not?"

Norman Klee, apparently more at ease now, replied, "Yes, I was. But a few years ago, rather than retire, I was persuaded to stay on at reduced hours, and pay. Without the title. I still pretty much oversee things down there. It's not a large office - only a few people now, most of whom, like myself, have been there a long time. No one seemed to want the added responsibility of managing the place. So, things just seemed to continue along as they always have."

Being well versed in how Tribal offices are often run, Charlie had to smile at this. "So, and correct me if I'm wrong, you would have come up for retirement during the time Erwin Johnson worked here?"

A look crossed the man's face, not a look of surprise exactly, but rather a combination of that and a sudden wariness. "Yes...that's right. He wasn't there long though, before he was put in charge. The man seemed to have friends in high places, if you know what I mean?"

Charlie nodded and motioned him to go on.

"It was Erwin who first suggested I stay on, saying he had need of someone who knew how the system worked to help ease his transition, you know. The truth is, Mr. Yazzie, I really couldn't afford to quit anyway. My wife and I were struggling back then. I thought myself lucky to have the opportunity to keep something coming in."

"What did you think of Erwin Johnson—personally, I mean, and just between the two of us?"

"Oh, he was alright at first, pretty much let me run things as I had in the past. He would come in some afternoons and ask to see certain files which he would take to his office, saying he needed to come up to speed on how things worked around here."

"You wouldn't happen to still have a file on Johnson, himself, would you?"

Norman stiffened visibly yet answered calmly enough. "The fact is, Mr. Yazzie, those files disappeared about the same time as Mr. Johnson left his position here. It was a first for us, and only showed up in an audit sometime later. Nothing was ever done about it as far as I know." He thought a moment before going on, "There is, I believe, still an employee profile on the man in Personnel. I doubt he had access to that. I could ask them if you like."

"Well, that's good to know. I may want you to send that up to me this afternoon." Charlie moved a few papers around on his desk and then asked, "Norman, I wonder if you could tell me something. How long after the big Tribal corruption scandal happened, did Erwin actually leave your office?"

The old man thought only a moment before answering, "Almost immediately, I suppose. Maybe even before. Things were pretty chaotic around here at the time. No one really seemed to know what happened to Erwin. I, personally, have not seen or heard from the man since."

When Norman finished this last statement, Charlie introduced the question he intended asking from the beginning. "It's my understanding, Mr. Klee, Erwin Johnson was never charged in any wrongdoing during the Tribal corruption proceedings. How did you feel about that—off the record of course? This conversation is just between the two of us."

Norman Klee looked doubtful as he tightened his grip on the arm of the chair and leaned closer to the desk.

Moistening his lips with the tip of his tongue, he seemed to search for the proper words, eventually saying, "Everyone in this office thought, at the time, that Erwin Johnson *was* involved in what was going on with the Tribal Council." He paused and fixed Charlie with a nervous gaze. "But they were wrong, Mr. Yazzie." Slowly relaxing his grip on the chair, the old man turned his attention to the outer office window, watching the workers at their desks for a long moment before returning his gaze to the Investigator. "Erwin Johnson had his own thing going on here. There may have been others involved as well, but he was the major actor, as far as I could tell. To the best of my recollection, it was something that had been going on for several years. It is my opinion, that Erwin was already at it when he was with the legal team up there. It occurred to me back then, things may have been getting too hot for him in his previous position and this was the real reason for his move down to records. That, and the certain advantages our sector offered." The old man held up an open hand. "This was all well before your time here, Mr. Yazzie. It was about the time Legal Services was being flooded with requests for legal aid from ailing uranium miners and their families—compensation from those mining corporations here on the reservation. Our people had their advocacy groups of course, but they were small and ineffectual in the face of the government coverups. Not to mention the corporate media campaigns."

Charlie knew he was on to something now, but still didn't know exactly what it was he was looking at. "What, exactly, was Johnson doing, Norman?"

The old man sighed. "Well, I think it all started out innocently enough. A few of those miners were beginning to win class-action lawsuits, and some of these people came to Erwin for advice, to guide them through the initial process. Later, as I understand it, he helped them expedite the collection of what was coming to them. Some even asked his advice on what to do with their money once it was allocated." Here the old man stopped to wipe a hand across his eyes. "These were poor ignorant people, Mr. Yazzie - the sort who had no one else to turn to. I suspect it was at this point that Erwin devised a plan by which he could funnel their money into an investment account he had personally set up. He paid them their interest on time and even disbursed funds when someone needed extra cash for some little thing or another, but he always cautioned them to keep the bulk of their money in his fund, where it could continue earning interest for them. At that point, his investors were grateful for what he'd done for them and pleased to think they were doing the right thing for their families. I believe, as time went on, Erwin became more convinced he could get away with this indefinitely." The old man touched a hand to his chin. "He was a very smart man, Mr. Yazzie. Had things been a little different back then, he might have wound up a successful lawyer, even off the reservation, if you get my meaning?"

Charlie was very aware of how things were back then. When graduating law school, he had, himself, tried to land a job off the reservation, yet failed at every turn. Things *were* different back then. The Investigator sat dumbfounded at the audacity of Erwin Johnson's scheme — even more amazed that he had, thus far, gotten away with it.

"How did you come across this information, Norman?" Charlie said, hoping against hope the old man had not been involved in the scheme. "Did you know what was going on, Norman?"

"No, Mr. Yazzie, not until years later. You see, I attended a little New Mexico college, down south of here, where I earned a degree in accounting - Forensic Accounting actually, which is how I worked my way into a job at Legal Services. In those times, as you know, an Indian, even one with a degree, had a hard time finding a job in any professional occupation. My training made me suspicious of Erwin right from the beginning, but I never approached anyone about it. I couldn't afford to 'rock the boat' as they say. But, years later, old Isabell

Joe came to me. She thought her late husband had gotten himself mixed up in some sort of phony investment company - one involving Erwin Johnson. Well, then I could no longer turn a blind eye. Isabell's husband, William Joe, worked in our accounting department for years, and had only recently passed-away. Going through some of his things, Isabell ran across office paperwork that William had taken home to work on. There was something about it that looked fishy to her. I must tell you that Isabell was a smart lady in her own right. I'd known her since boarding school, and few put anything over on her, even back then. When she brought me the papers it was pretty clear to me then, what was going on. I felt bad I hadn't caught on to this before, but as I said, William was doing most all of this at home, for extra money, and I'll bet it wasn't much either."

Charlie stood up, hands clasped behind his back, he took a turn around the office, pausing to gaze at his framed Law Degree, as though seeing it for the first time.

The old man watched silently from his chair, possibly wondering what the Investigator was thinking. He couldn't know that Charlie's own Aunt, Annie Eagletree, had been a recipient of a rather large settlement some years before—after her husband died from what she called 'uranium poisoning'. She had not suffered the fate of those disadvantaged people Norman Klee was now describing. By reservation standards, Annie remained a wealthy woman still. She had, it seemed, been one of the lucky ones.

Chapter 13

The Evaluation

There comes, to every man, the occasional yet lingering suspicion he has misjudged a person. In Thomas Begay's case, prejudging a person—man, or woman— was a matter of instinct. Being the sort who put great stock in first impressions, he could seldom be swayed once he had settled on a person's perceived worth.

Lucy Tallwoman, on the other hand, was of a less suspicious nature, but she too, had second thoughts when it came to the young Sam Klah and his instant attraction to her daughter. Not that Sam wasn't a nice enough boy. He had proven himself stalwart and brave on the recent chase. While she supposed he was smart enough, considering his isolated upbringing, it still was hard to imagine him being able to support a wife or family in this modern world. When *she* was young, it was not uncommon for young people to marry at this age, but these days it was usually frowned upon by parents with certain aspirations for their children. It could be, that Sam's traditional upbringing had caused him to think he would be expected to move in with his new wife's family—as was proper in earlier times. Even now this would not be thought unusual in the more remote areas. Lucy knew her husband would, nonetheless, have a hard time with it.

Still, it brought a smile to remember that Thomas himself had moved in with *her* after her own daughter left him. He was not that much older than Sam at the time—and with little better prospects than the boy. Throw in Thomas's drinking problem, and she could understand why her father was against him from the start. The two had, in fact, only recently come to more equitable terms. She wasn't likely to bring any of this up, of course—Thomas being the way he was and all.

While both Lucy and her husband came from a traditional background, they had, of late, fallen into a more modern lifestyle, letting go of the old ways to some extent. Admittedly, they were not as progressive in their thinking as Charlie Yazzie's family, but then they'd had old Paul T'Sosi to contend with, keeping them aligned with the Beauty Path as it were. The odd thing to her, was that educated Charlie Yazzie, over the years, had gradually become more comfortable with the old ways.

Thomas and herself had drifted in somewhat the opposite direction. That was the reservation for you. The outside world might change, but here there would always be that magnetic pull back to center.

Ida Marie will soon be of age, Lucy thought, as will the boy. Then they will do what they will do with little thought to the consequences. And so, of course, life would treat them accordingly. Lucy Tallwoman pondered these things without the slightest hint of malice and, in the end, was satisfied life was unfolding as it should—or at least, that there was very little she, or Thomas, could do about it.

~~~~~~

Paul T'Sosi sat just in front of his *hogan,* warming his bones in the sun. It was the *hogan* his daughter had been born in. He thought it a shame the sun would only be on his bench for a few hours this morning, not the greater part of the day, as it once had. The new house Thomas built, now shaded the old *hogan* nearly all day. This was no bad a thing in the heat of summer, something Thomas was quick to point out when the old man groused about it. But now, in the early days of Autumn there was no justifying it. Not to Paul T'Sosi.

This thing with Ida Marie's new boyfriend had him thinking of late. The upshot was he had promised the girl he would see if he couldn't find where the boy had been hidden away—if that was even possible. Paul was curious what kind of boy this was. An exceptional one should his granddaughter be any judge—which he somewhat doubted, not having any previous boyfriend to compare him to.

Thomas had taken his wife and son to town to see the dentist. Ida Marie had gone the week before and was pronounced fine—apart from one small cavity. She had Sue Yazzie's insistence on dental hygiene to thank for that. Lucy Begay had, for some time now, been concerned with the state of everyone's teeth, insisting it was not something they could ignore. Her father had 'remarkably good teeth for his age', she said, meaning the few he had left. The old man himself summed things up by declaring he was not a big believer in putting new chrome on an old bumper.

Lucy told her father they most likely wouldn't be back until evening. She wanted to do some shopping after their appointments and would leave her truck in case 'something happened'.

Paul knew where she kept the keys—should there be such an emergency. Not that she intended her old father to do the driving. She knew Ida Marie was capable enough for emergency service. The girl had completed her driver's education program at school, with high marks, but her father still was holding off on her getting a car of her own—even more so now that Sam Klah had entered the picture.

~~~~~~

Giving the family time to be well down the road, Paul opened the kitchen door a crack, whispered, "Psst, psst." The girl was waiting and came on the run. Ida Marie had her permit for almost a year and, though still not a confident driver, was proficient enough to get around the reservation—should she be accompanied by an adult driver. She had not yet braved Farmington traffic.

On the way to the truck, the girl passed Paul in long strides, quickly putting her a good way ahead. Jumping in, she started the engine threw open the passenger side door for her old grandfather, who still was only halfway to the pickup. Breathing hard, the old man came up saying, "Take it easy now, girl, we're not going to a fire you know. It will be hours before the others get back. Let's slow this thing down and not get a ticket our first time out." He smiled over at her as he caught his breath and with a satisfied grin, said, "I know where this Sam Klah fellow is."

"How did you find out, Gramps?"

"I decided to make a few phone calls yesterday when everyone was busy. I got lucky on the first one, too." He chuckled to himself. "Ponyboy residence,' that's how they answer the phone over there now. I have to laugh every time I hear it."

"Harley Ponyboy told you where Sam is?"

"No, I didn't have to ask big Harley. It was little Harley who answered the phone. That boy don't usually say a whole hell of a lot, but this time he was chattering away like a Magpie." The old man chortled to himself. "That little boy can talk just fine when he wants to. He right away started telling me how he'd been to see Doc and got a free sucker. That's what he said, 'a *free* sucka,' as though George might sometimes charge for them. He couldn't stop talking, telling me he got the 'las' one, too.' Then he whispered to me that he thinks Sam has been eating most of them when Doc isn't looking."

"Ha, so that's where they've been hiding him. I should have known. I'll bet everyone already knows except me."

Paul frowned. "Well, I didn't know, but I do now, and no one's the wiser either." He threw Ida a sly look.

"Do you think your driving skills are up to taking a little run over there? It's in Farmington, you know?"

Ida didn't have to think about it. "You bet I am. I know right where he lives, and it's on this side of town—easy to get to. It won't be any problem at all." The girl sounded excited as she reached over and patted Paul's shoulder. "Thanks, Gramps, I won't forget this. And I'll make it up to you. You can count on that!"

"I am counting on it. I've been wanting some of those oatmeal cookies you make, and this seemed like a good way to get some." He was smiling as he said this, but he meant it, too.

~~~~~~

In her excitement, Ida Marie talked the entire way into town, all the while running the gamut of radio stations, and jacking up the volume before twirling the knob from one station to another. By the time the girl approached Professor Custer's place, Paul T'Sosi thought he might have to pry his fingers off the dash. It had been all he could do not to have her pull over and take the wheel himself. It had been an eventful drive and he forced himself not to dwell on the inevitable trip home.

The girl surprised the old man by whipping the pickup into a parallel parking space with the aplomb of one long experienced in the maneuver, barely bumping the car in front. As Paul got down from the truck, he heaved a sigh of relief saying, "Good job, my girl. That Driver's Ed course you took must have had a very good teacher. One with nerves of steel."

With a smug glance at her grandfather, Ida admitted, "I only got a C in driving but he gave me an A in parking."

"Well, I've seldom seen it done any better." Peering up at the house the old man thought he saw someone at the window, but it was just for an instant and he couldn't be sure.

Ida Marie was looking in the rearview mirror, patting her hair into place before giving her lips a brisk rub to bring a little color. Smiling at herself she canted her face to one side, apparently satisfied she had done all she could do.

The Professor's house sat well back from the street, on a large corner lot, and now served as his place of business as well. When business began falling off the previous winter, he'd given up his small office space in town. Now he made do with two outbuildings at the rear of the property to house his work. He was of an age to retire and said he had thought about it from time to time but couldn't quite bring himself to make the transition. Still, there were projects of his own he'd kept on the back burner. Paul knew Doc worried he might not have time left to work those in, even with his reduced involvement in the archaeological survey—and sometimes salvage business.

It was the Professor himself, who opened the door at their first knock. "Well, well, well. Look who we have here." He ushered them into the house with a slight bow and huge smile of welcome. "Come into the kitchen. I was about to have a cup of coffee." A momentary look of concern passed over his face as he turned to lead the way, but it was gone before he offered them seats. The Professor busied himself with the coffee making, still casting covert glances through the window towards the outbuildings.

His guests sat watching, as he brought out an elaborate French press from its alcove by the refrigerator. "This is the latest thing in coffee making, at least here in the colonies, it is." He smiled at the pair sitting solemn faced at the table. They obviously had failed to grasp the humor in the comment. That or it wasn't really that funny.

Ida Marie knew the professor was having a little joke but saw her Grandfather was taking it all quite seriously, showing a definite interest in the method.

Coffee was a great favorite of Paul's as it was for most Navajo, and the thought of a new way of preparing it was intriguing. He'd not heard of such a thing and was instantly drawn to the possibilities.

Doc already had the water boiling but added a rough-ground mix of dark roasted beans to the contraption before pouring in the hot water.

Paul rose slightly from his chair, the better to see the operation.

"This will only take about four minutes to brew." The Professor, obviously fond of the device, smiled at the two of them, "This way of making coffee has been around in Europe since the twenties, but just now seems to be catching on over here. I have to admit I've become addicted." He held up a finger. "I think you are going to like this, Paul. You too, Ida, if you are allowed coffee?"

Paul spoke up, "This girl has been drinking coffee since before she could ride a bike."

Bringing the coffee maker to the table George put the palm of his hand on the plunger and slowly pressed it down into the carafe, isolating the grounds at the bottom of the clear glass reservoir. The aroma filled the room, and the Professor beamed as he went to the cupboard.

Paul nodded his admiration of the process as he leaned in to examine the results. "Well, isn't this something?" he asked Ida Marie.

George came back with cups, along with sugar and cream. Setting a cup in front of each, he poured the fragrant brew before sitting down. He seemed satisfied with the impression he'd made on his old friend. They each fixed their coffee according to their own particular liking. Paul was first to take a sip. The old singer smiled across the table and smacked his lips to show his approval.

Ida Marie took a dainty taste and added her approval as well. The girl continually glanced around the room looking for some sign that Sam had been there. She was fairly bursting with questions but was determined not to barge into the older men's prelude to the real discussion. It is not the Navajo way—to come directly to the point in a conversation, thinking it important to judge the other person's mood before getting to the crux of the matter. She had been around her grandfather long enough to know better than interrupt his carefully contrived approach to the subject. George Custer, also familiar with this traditional form of dancing around the point of a conversation before addressing the main purpose of the talk.

The men enjoyed their coffee, chatting about the possibility of Paul finding a French press locally. In a nation of serious coffee drinkers, the fulsome brew had, over the years, taken on a near ceremonial significance for the Navajo. The Begay household would soon be on track to own the first French press coffee maker on the reservation. The *Diné* had come a long way from those first dispersals of coffee beans in their Government rations. Not knowing what they were, they had been boiled and eaten like any other beans. The resulting digestive illnesses, and even a few deaths, might have put the people off the drink for all time. Eventually, however, with proper preparation, the exact opposite came about, and coffee became an essential commodity for the *Diné*.

George Custer sat back, obviously enjoying his cup, as he gazed across the table. "So, I'm sure you two didn't come here just so Ida Marie could practice her driving."

Paul T'Sosi cradled his cup in both hands and, looking to his granddaughter, encouraged the girl with a lift of his chin, indicating she should be the one to go first.

Ida had always been a straight talker, and looked George straight in the eye, just as a white person might. "Professor Custer, we would like to know where we can find Sam Klah. We think he is here, and if he is, I would like to see him for a few minutes, if that's possible? I know you are not supposed to tell anyone, but I have to know." The girl, now visibly trembling, blurted out, "I need to talk to him. It can't wait."

George looked over at Paul T'Sosi and saw the same question in his eyes. Turning to Ida, he carefully set down his cup and clasped his hands together in front of him, rubbing his knuckles as though working out how best to approach the thing.

"Harley Ponyboy called last night. I know little Harley told you Sam was here, but that was yesterday." George raised an eyebrow at Paul T'Sosi and pursed his lips for a moment. "That's no longer true. The boy left early this morning with Harley, who has given his word he would tell no one where the boy's been taken. It's important for you to know, Ida, that Sam's life is in serious danger. This is currently the only way to protect him. Until we can find out who has made these attempts on his life, the boy will have to remain in hiding." He fixed the girl with a long and soulful gaze before going on. "I'm sorry this had to play out this way, but there is just no other way to go about it."

Ida Marie's breath caught in her throat. "But...how long will it be before I can see him again?"

"I wish I knew, but what I can tell you is that Charlie Yazzie and Billy Red Clay are working nonstop to find out who's behind this. Not to mention, the FBI as well. Thanks to Charlie and Billy, they have some promising leads to go on. I can also tell you, this move was not what Sam wanted, but he understood the need for it and agreed to try it before taking off on his own. It's important you know that moving him didn't happen because you found out where he was. This plan has been in the works for days and would have happened no matter what." The Professor sighed and turned his palms up in a gesture of futility. "Ida, it was only a matter of time before someone spotted him here in town. We couldn't allow that to happen." The Professor paused, seeing tears glistening in the girl's eyes. Hesitating only a moment, he pulled a creased envelope from his back pocket and handed it to her. "Sam left this letter for you, Ida. I promised I would see you got it."

The girl thanked the Professor and, taking the letter, held it tightly to her as she turned to her grandfather with a look that made the old man sad.

"Come along then, Granddaughter, let's see if we can't get home before the family gets back and catches us gone." So saying, the pair made their goodbyes to George Custer and made their way back to the truck - Ida Marie sniffling into a tissue. Old man Paul T'Sosi already dreading the drive home, patted the girl's arm and offered to do the driving.

R. Allen Chappell

Chapter 14

Deception

Erwin Johnson's self-exile had, over the years, brought with it few regrets. His own final judgement was that his had not been a life well spent, nor had it been a particularly honorable one. For one who started with such high ideals and worked hard to attain the necessary tools to do better, he had often fallen miserably short. Through it all, however, he convinced himself he had, at least, been of some useful service to those who put their trust in him. Guiding these unfortunates through the pitfalls of filing their claims had been hard work, but undeniably fulfilling at the same time. Granted, the wrongs inflicted by greedy uranium interests, acting under the auspices of an unseeing Government—deserved exactly what they got, and more.

There was, of course, the undeniable fact much of the moneys collected eventually came to reside in his own pocket. He liked to think, in retrospect, that his 'stewardship' of those funds was to the good of those uneducated people who would probably have squandered it on alcohol, new pickup trucks, and other such foolish self-indulgences. At least under his guidance their windfalls had become a self-sustaining fund from which they could draw in time of need, assuming those needs were reasonable, and that the end result would not deplete the general fund to any great extent.

Using a portion of the money from new investments, to cover the interest and small withdrawals necessary to sustain the integrity of the fund, Erwin Johnson successfully managed to perpetuate one of the oldest and more profitable of all investment scams. One that had duped much more sophisticated people than these on the reservation.

When the ongoing turmoil over Tribal corruption charges finally overwhelmed the Prosecution, whose resources ultimately proved to be limited in both manpower and funding, Erwin decided the time was right to make his exit. Take some time out perhaps, to enjoy the fruits of his considerable labor.

Taking with him every vestige of records, and other information which might tie him to any related wrongdoing. Erwin found refuge in the most remote part of the reservation. It was the part where he was born and raised... *Tsé Bii' Ndzigaii.* Taking up his old tribal name he spent the next several years carving out a snug place for himself, bringing the work along slowly so as not to attract undue attention. The property, belonging to his long dead parents, was his now by virtue of rights common to the unspoken law of that land.

He lived alone, and with little social interaction among his widely scattered neighbors. The one exception to this self-imposed exile was Lyla Etcitty, now going by her married name, Lyla Klah. Though her husband succumbed to that deadly malady so common among uranium miners. The woman moved only a short distance away, to a place thought to be safe, and for years lived alone there with her young son.

Over a period of time, Erwin and Lyla's relationship had caused talk, though no one could say exactly what that relationship was. It was only then that Lyla let it slip that the legal suit, on behalf of her late husband, had finally worked its way through the courts. The upshot being she would likely be in line for a considerable settlement. She didn't know when this would happen, but she had somehow arrived at the conclusion she must remain on her own until the money was disbursed. Erwin had already been aware some of these early suits were being processed, at long last, and that some of the awards were staggering. By virtue of his experience with the ins and outs of the business, he was quick to offer his guidance, helping her through the final process, assuring her he would be able to increase the amount considerably. As time wore on, Erwin had become increasingly insistent he be allowed to handle the matter for her. While Lyla had never been a worldly person, she did have a certain 'woman's intuition' when it came to men, refusing to be pushed into a situation she felt had gone somewhat awry.

In the ensuing weeks, the two of them had continued to argue over Erwin's offer of help. He had even gone so far as to suggest moving in to take care of her and the boy. Lyla, however, remained adamant, and eventually ordered him off the place. It was a move he was forced to admit was her traditional right, though he had no saddle she could set outside the door to signal his exit. He went away peaceably enough, but forever after harbored a smoldering grudge that lasted until the day Lyla Klah died. And it was then Erwin Johnson began studying what was left for him to do.

~~~~~

Even after Erwin managed to survive the Statute of Limitations regarding most of his previous wrong doings, he was forced to admit that lying-low had come at a price.

His resources had dwindled to an alarming degree over the years and, while he was careful to maintain a lifestyle that could only be considered as minimal, there had been those other expenses. Certain people had been involved in his early ventures and they were also feeling the pinch. As might be expected, their silence didn't come cheap. Growing desperate, Erwin had eventually explored more devious options.

He had, over the years, taken great pains to keep himself apprised of the status of Lyla Klah's claim against the now-defunct mining companies. A claim so undeniable, it was accepted by the Federal Government and slowly gained traction. It had recently been approved for settlement. Still, there had not yet been a payoff, and while it was not uncommon for an award to languish in the turgid backwaters of Government bureaucracy, often for years, there was little doubt Lyla's death would now further muddy the waters. Erwin, however, was not a man to be easily discouraged. Oddly enough, he felt this was exactly the sort of complication that might play in his favor—should the cards happen to fall just right. Legally speaking, the next in line to claim the money would be young Sam Klah, and barring that, Lyla's younger brother John.

John Etcitty, a person Erwin had fervently hoped never to see again, would now have to be part of his plan. From Etcitty's earliest years, it was generally agreed he was somewhat 'unsettled in his thinking' as his own people delicately chose to put it. What he really was, according to Erwin, was a psychopath, who either, didn't know right from wrong, or just plain didn't care.

~~~~~~~

By the time he was eighteen, John Etcitty had been involved in several unprovoked, and serious, assaults in the reservation's backcountry. 'Back of the back' as some called it. The second incident had ended in the lingering and painful death of one of his own relatives. It was at this point, the man was declared by his clan to be *Yóó'á hááskahh* or, 'one who is lost'. Shunned even by his own family, he was forced to go underground, ranging for years in the far canyons. Places so rugged very few people, Indian or white, had ever set foot.

Those few determined whites, uranium prospectors for the most part, who were tough enough...or greedy enough to enter that isolated country knew they did so at the risk of their lives. In the early days of the boom some of these men, loners mostly, did disappear, never to be seen again. Much of this because of the attempts of outsiders to find even the smallest, isolated deposits of Yellow Dirt, many no more than a pickup load, but sometimes rich enough to make a man wealthy—depending, on his definition of the term.

The larger commercial mines were more often open pit, or the more dangerous underground mines. Both operations left huge amounts of tailings in their wake. Even sophisticated people were sometimes ignorant of the dangerous effects.

In many places across the Four Corners, contractors hauled in dump-truck loads of these waste products to be used as landfill for homes and businesses to be built on. The effects are still being felt today, with Government remediation efforts still ongoing after decades.

This was the country where John Etcitty was still spoken of, but only in whispers, and never by his real name. Someone might say, 'You remember that man who was a brother to the woman who lived over there behind Big Mesa...the one who died of Yellow Dirt poison? Well, my cousin thinks he saw him last week when he was hunting a lost horse...over past Hidden Springs...you know that place? Did you hear the man only has one eye now? That's what the people are saying up there where he's from. I do know he was a hell of a tracker when he was young, everyone says so...maybe he still is...I don't know. But I wouldn't want him on *my* trail. They say when he is in his crazy head, he might kill a person for a drink of water—even if he was standing right there by the spring. That's the kind of man they say he is now.'

Those were the sort of stories told around the fires at night. When the little ones were fast asleep.

Chapter 15

The Problem

For some time now, Harley Ponyboy had reckoned there were some sort of added precautions he should be taking. There was the new security system, of course, but he didn't really understand all that he should about operating it. Maybe he would have Charlie go over it with him again the next time he was over. That rattlesnake in the mailbox surprise had been preying on his mind, and was, in fact, becoming the focus of his dreams—even the wakeful hours that followed. Little Harley was being kept inside for the most part, and he figured he'd probably been allowing him more television time than he rightfully should.

There had been no TV when Harley was his son's age, not where he'd lived anyway. And while he admittedly enjoyed time spent watching cartoons with the boy, he knew it wasn't all that good for either of them.

They would probably be better off outdoors. It was discouraging for him to think he'd gradually let this thing take over their lives. They saw the Yazzie's on a regular basis, of course, and knew Charlie's family was committed to keeping a watchful eye out for them. Still, he couldn't help thinking there was something more he might be doing to keep his son safe. But safe from what, or who? That was the root of the question. No one could yet say who was behind the attempts on young Sam Klah, or even how he himself may have been the target of the would-be killer. He knew Charlie and Billy Red Clay were using every investigative means at their disposal, and that the FBI had taken a stronger hand as well, but still nothing seemed to be pointing in any particular direction, none at all as far as he could see.

Charlie occasionally reminded him that Erwin Johnson was still under the scrutiny of those working the case, and also assured him everything possible was being done in that regard. Eventually, he said, someone would run across the boy's Uncle, John Etcitty, cautioning that he might have something to do with the mystery. In the meantime, the Legal Services Investigator had advised Harley and his son they should just stay home as much as possible. "It's just a matter of time, Harley. We'll get a handle on this sooner or later, and everything can get back to normal."

I must be getting old, Harley thought as the gorge rose in his throat. *I have never been one to sit around waiting for someone else to fight my battles. Maybe this big house and the money has made me soft. Maybe I'm starting to be afraid inside. That's not me. That's not who I want to be! Someday my son might look back on this and think bad of me for not getting out there and taking the bull by the horns.*

Harley looked in on his son, watching a moment as the colorful characters scampered across the TV screen to make the boy smile. And it was then that his heart filled with rage at who he was becoming, and he growled to himself through clinched teeth, "I am Harley Ponyboy... Enough is enough!"

~~~~~~

Thomas Begay had just turned up the drive and slowed his truck when Harley Jr. came running around the corner of the house. His father was right behind him, arms loaded with camping gear.

Pulling up behind the pair, Thomas slid out of the truck, stretched his lanky frame, and approached the Harleys with a curious glance at the loaded pickup. "What? Did you sell the house?"

Harley looked around as though he hadn't heard the man coming, which would have been impossible given the clatter of Thomas's diesel truck. He sighed heavily and shook his head. "No, I didn't sell the house...I'm just going on a little road trip, that's all."

"Oh. Are you taking little Iron Pants here, along with you?" The boy glowered at the tall Navajo. Although Thomas was one of his favorite people, he didn't like the name he'd been called and didn't hesitate to show it.

Harley, throwing his load of assorted tack and camping gear into the truck bed, faced his friend with a grimace. "He's goin' to stay with the Yazzie's for a couple days. Sue said they would be happy to have him. She misses having him around, she said."

Still frowning, the boy looked up at his father with a defiant shake of his head, blurting out, "No, I ain't, I not go'n to Sue's house."

Harley glared at the boy but kept his tone of voice even and calm. "Uh...yes you are Junior. We already been through this twice this morning and this is the last time I'm telling you." He shook a finger at the boy but still didn't raise his voice, not as much as he probably wanted to. "Unless you want a good paddling you better just pipe down, young man."

Thomas smiled. He had, of late, become more and more suspicious that the child had taken after his mother. A woman known to be rudely outspoken and seriously opinionated. He was thinking how odd it was that each of Harley Ponyboy's two previous choices in women were of a kind—neither anything at all like the easy-going man himself.

The boy in the meantime had drawn back a booted little foot as though to kick at his father. Harley quickly held up a hand. "Do you remember what happened the last time you tried that?"

The boy puffed up like a toad, giving his father a fierce look, but then his face fell and he only scuffed the boot in the dirt.

Harley squatted down in front of him. "Junior. You are going to Sue's. I have something to do, and I won't have time to keep track of you while I'm doing it, and that's that!"

This little conversation was about as rough as Thomas had ever seen the man be with his son, and it was almost immediately obvious that he regretted it. Harley had never been one to let his temper get away with him, and this was a sure indicator of how much pressure he was under.

Thomas chuckled a moment as he watched the pair and then quickly changed the subject. "Where you headed, Harley?" He gave a push of his chin toward the loaded truck. "Looks like you might be off to a camp job somewhere?" He'd seen the saddle leaned up against the front of the bed, a set of panniers arranged to hold it in place. "You going up to help Doc for a few days?" He didn't really think so, or he'd have heard about it by now, and that alone was worrying him.

Harley slammed the tailgate shut and faced the tall Navajo. "It's none of your damned business where I'm going, big boy, so quit asking. I'm going to be gone a few days, that's all."

Thomas still smiling, nodded at this. "I just thought you might want a little company, that's all. I don't have anything to do the next few days. I wouldn't mind riding along."

Harley's frown softened slightly, but he didn't look up when he said, "I doubt you could keep up where I'm going."

Thomas chuckled knowing his friend didn't believe that for a moment. "Well, if I see I can't make it, I'll just turn around and come on home. How about that?" and then, "Which way you headed, anyhow?"

Harley looked down and smoothed a gouge in the dirt with the toe of a boot. "Up on the *Tsé Bii' Ndzigaii...* I guess...or thereabouts.*"

"Ahh, well then, you'll be passing right by our place on the way. I'll just scoot on up there and be ready to leave when you come by."

The two men stared at one another for a moment. Harley nodded and, without another word, turned back to his work. As he watched Thomas Begay turn onto the highway, there was the beginning of a smile on his face. He looked down at his son, now busy dragging his own little saddle up to the truck. Harley took the saddle and set it aside. "Maybe another time you can go, Harley. Right now, though, you need to go over to Sue's with me." And then taking the boy by the hand he started up the lane to the Yazzie house. Harley was reminded how much his son was like him at this age, and this pleased him. He figured the boy was going to be alright.

Harley wished the child's mother had lived to see how big he was getting. She hadn't been much of a mother, really, but when the chips were down, she'd stood up for him, and paid for it with her life. That had to count for something.

~~~~~~

When he saw Harley's truck coming, Thomas stepped up next to the Highway, horse saddled and gear bag beside him. The red Chevy pulled a four-horse trailer behind it, with bales of hay tied to the fenders. The trailer brakes locked up as the truck slid to a stop on the loose gravel in front of the mailbox. The driver eased it forward until the back of the trailer came even with the man. Thomas noted the white-poly water tank, crosswise in the manger up front. He didn't know what the little guy was planning, but figured he was, for damn sure, ready for it. Thomas opened the rear gate to a chorus of braying mules, clucking to encourage his horse to bump a long-ears out of the way he smiled as it bulled its way in amongst them. He knew mules will seldom argue with a horse. Raised by mares, their earliest experiences tells them horses are the dominate creature on any manure pile.

Slamming the trailer gate closed, Thomas picked up his bulging duffle and grunted as he hefted the bag onto his shoulder and moved up to the pickup bed, easing it over the tailgate.

Harley flung open the passenger door for him, and Thomas settled into his seat, holding his coat and a 30-30 saddle gun.

Harley glanced over at the rifle. "Expecting trouble?"

Thomas didn't say anything but reached in his belt to pull out a revolver he then stuffed in the glove box.

Grinning he declared, "I was afraid you might have forgot your lucky rabbit's foot."

They remained silent for the first twenty miles, but both men flinched when an old dog coyote jumped in front of the truck. The lucky canine barely avoided being run over. With a loaded four horse trailer behind him, Harley hadn't bothered to hit the brakes.

"Funny time a day for that rascal to be out running around." Thomas looked in his side mirror in time to catch a glimpse of the animal scooting down an arroyo. "Well, you know how it is...places to go, things to do." He looked over at his old friend. "Speaking of which, are we just on a little vacation out here, or have you got more serious business in mind?"

The little man muttered, "Why? You afraid you didn't bring enough bullets?"

Harley had a look on his face that reminded Thomas of their drinking days. There had been a time when he and Harley were well acquainted with the small-town Indian bars bordering the reservation. Together, they had drank and fought their way through a good many of them. Turning to peer out the window, the taller man couldn't help grinning at the memories he saw staring back at him. Those times were behind them now, but they continued to watch out for each other - both with the realization they were only one drink away from being right back where they started.

Thomas had already guessed they were going into the 'back of the back', as it was known in some quarters, and was already aware who they were looking for. It suited him just fine and was overdue to his way of thinking. He'd grown tired of listening to Charlie Yazzie talk about how he and Billy Red Clay were making progress *It is time to take the bull by the horns.*

Chapter 16

The Chance

It was late afternoon when Harley's dust-covered Chevy turned north onto a barely distinguishable track through the cedars. The camp they were heading to had been here since before he was born. Fifty-sixty years, at least, and probably even more. His Grandfather had told him that no one really knew where these people came from, but once settled here, they never left.

Harley adjusted the sun-visor slightly to shield the glare of the afternoon sun. Wrestling the rig up the rocky track, he found it necessary to slow to little more than a walk to avoid beating up the stock. He watched as Thomas grew increasingly impatient with the delay, despite knowing there was no way around it. "Eldon's place is just over this next hill if I remember right. I been knowing this old man all my life. He's been in this country longer than anyone. If the person we are looking for is anywhere near here, Eldon Bitsui will know of it."

"Well, I'm glad to hear it," Thomas said, dryly, "I just love it when a plan comes together." Readjusting his gangly frame, he squirmed in his seat as the truck jounced side to side. "I need to stretch my legs. I'll bet those animals back there could use a break, too. All this bouncing around has likely wore the ears off those mules."

When they topped the rise, Thomas was somewhat taken aback to see a camp so well situated in this barren country. A long pool of water lay at the head of an otherwise dry creek bed. The water disappeared underground in less than a hundred yards—not unusual in this country—and would likely reappear farther downstream. Well built corrals of heavy cedar posts lined the lower section of the creek, and a small orchard of peach and apricot trees, some with fruit still on them, was growing on the piece of flat ground along the creek bed. He noted the thin stream of irrigation water feeding the trees, wishing his own place was so lucky. The fenced upper portion of the little canyon was well grassed, as though they might be saving it for winter. A large cedar-log *hogan,* expertly chinked with mud and shredded cedar bark, sat on a slightly elevated bench. An ancient Jeep pickup, looking as though it might still run, was parked in the yard where two good sized stock dogs stood at attention near the door. There was a white feather of smoke rising from the chimney.

Thomas grinned. "Looks like someone still lives here alright. I hope it's who you think it is."

Harley pulled the truck up beside the corrals and shut off the engine. Glancing over at the enclosures, he shook his head. "Looks to me like only one of those pens has seen much use lately. Maybe, they haven't brought their stock down from summer pasture yet." He squinted up the canyon. "This old man used to run a goodly number of sheep, back in day."

"What are those dogs doing down here then?" Thomas asked, calculating how aggressive they might prove to be, and mentally preparing himself for evasive action, should it become necessary.

"This old man has always kept a lot of dogs. Good-bred dogs, too." Harley beeped the horn for courtesy's sake, and both men got down from the truck to stretch, all the while keeping a wary eye on the ever-watchful dogs. At least they were the only ones about, as far as they could see. Staying close to the truck and keeping a polite distance between them and the *hogan,* they waited another moment or two. Then Harley reached through the open window, this time giving a good blast of the horn, thinking *maybe the old man has grown hard of hearing.*

The dogs glanced nervously toward the door this time. They too, it seemed, expected better of their master. Still, neither of the animals barked or moved a single step from where they were when the truck had pulled up. Thomas looked over at Harley, about to ask what he thought, when the *hogan* door opened with an audible screech, and an old man appeared in the opening, with one hand still on the latch. He obviously couldn't see well, shading his eyes with one hand as he peered into the late afternoon sun, to get a better look at his visitors.

"*Yaa'eh t'eeh* Harley called, with a raised hand and a smile. "How are you Eldon?"

The old man cocked his head to one side asking in old Navajo, "Is that you Harley Ponyboy?" He cupped a hand to one ear. "It sounds like you, all right."

Harley walked toward the man, with Thomas trailing behind. The two dogs took a step toward them, and the old man, without looking their way, made a noise deep in his throat that caused them to back up a step, while remaining vigilant, ears ticked forward.

As Harley drew nearer, the old man waved a greeting, motioning to the dogs they should stand down. Crestfallen, the pair withdrew to the side of the *hogan* where they each turned a full circle on the hard packed clay before lying down, heads on their paws, but not taking their eyes off the strangers.

Harley clapped Eldon on the shoulder and shook his hand as the old man, smiling now, leaned forward to stare at him, saying, "I was beginning to think I would never see you again, Harley Ponyboy. It has been a lot of years since you last came to see me." Then, looking past him, he studied Thomas for a moment before venturing, "I don't believe I know this other fellow. Who might he be? Ask him to come up here, where I can get a good look at him."

"This is my old friend, Thomas Begay. He likes to ride around with me when I go visiting."

Thomas came forward to shake hands, saying he had heard a lot about him from Harley, and was glad to finally make his acquaintance.

Reaching behind him, Eldon opened the door wider, insisting they come in for some coffee so they might sit down and be comfortable as they talked.

Inside the *hogan,* Thomas nodded approvingly at how neat and clean everything was. The dirt floor was freshly swept, and the table was covered with a well-scrubbed red-and-white checkered oil cloth. It looked to him as though the old man might have a wife. Eldon ladled water from a bucket into a huge coffee pot and then opened the stove door to stir the fire to life, sending a whisp of aromatic cedar to linger in the air.

The old man then turned to his guests, again motioning them to sit at the table. "Make yourself at home, you boys. I'll only be a few more minutes with this coffee, and then we can talk."

Harley guessed the old man needed to be close by to carry on any sort of meaningful conversation.

It was plain the man didn't have many visitors these days, and that he was eager to hear what news they might have.

Later, over coffee, he allowed it was too late for them to continue their travels, being so close to dark. It was a dangerous road at night he insisted. So, they might as well unload their animals and stay a while. They could put their stock in his corrals, he offered, or let them out in the upper pasture for a little green stuff, whichever they thought best. "The fences are still good up there. We try to keep up with such things, even though we haven't got much stock anymore."

Thomas raised his eyebrows at Harley, to see if he would consider staying the night.

Pursing his lips in consideration, Harley nodded, indicating he thought this might be a good idea.

Thomas, then taking it upon himself to see to their stock, took his leave, saying he thought the pasture would be best, as their animals might be a little sore after the rough ride. He figured a good roll in the grass might be just the thing to limber them up.

When they were alone, Eldon looked toward the little wood framed window overlooking the corrals. "My daughter should be back with the sheep before dark, and then we will fix something to eat."

Harley looked up in surprise. "I don't remember you having a daughter, Eldon."

"Well, I do." The old man chuckled, "She was probably away at boarding school back when you used to come around." He scratched his head. "Later, she worked in *Kayenta* for a while, so she wasn't around much then, either. She only came back when I got sick, and my eyesight got to where I couldn't take care of the place." The old man sighed, looking down, and rubbing the backs of his hands before continuing. "She doesn't really like it out here," he said, as he rose to pour them both some coffee. "But she says she will stay as long as I need her. She is a good daughter, strong and a hard worker. I'm happy to have her here, but of course, I know it won't be forever." He pursed his lips and gazed thoughtfully at Harley a moment before going on. "I think she would be about your age. Are you not married Harley?" He said this last, with an unpresuming look of curiosity.

Harley gave some thought to the question before answering. "No, I'm not married, Eldon. I was once, but she is gone now. "I do have a son, though, so it's just me and him, you know." He didn't say more, leaving it at this to avoid explaining the complicated turns his life had taken since last they'd met.

The old man, sensing Harley's reluctance to dwell on these things, nodded as though he understood and asked, "So, what really brings you out this way Harley? As I have said, I'm happy to see you, but it's a long rough way out here and I would hope you have a better reason to come than just to visit an old man." He lowered an eyelid in a sly wink. "Is there something I can do for you, Harley?" Though most elderly people in that country tend to approach the point of a conversation in a more roundabout fashion, Eldon Bitsui was not one of these. He thought he no longer had time enough to waste on beating about the bush. He was known to be a plain talker, who preferred to make his thoughts clear early on.

Harley leaned forward and, even though he knew Thomas wouldn't be back for a while, cast a glance at the door, as if there might be someone else lurking out there in the dark. "We're looking for someone, Eldon, a person you might know something about. You used to know everyone in this country and heard things no one else did."

The old man drew back in his chair, fixing his guest with a pensive stare, before cautiously admitting this was so. "There are very few around here I don't know, that much is true." And then, as though reading Harley's thoughts, added, "There have always been one or two out here we don't speak of, with good reason, but you know all about that." Eldon looked away for moment, wondering just how much more he should say. "I'm guessing this person you are looking for might be one of those...a witch, maybe?"

Now it was Harley's turn to look away. Softly he said, "From what I've heard, I suspect he might well be a witch of some sort."

The old man sank back into his chair and sighed from somewhere deep inside. "What name does this person go by? Keeping in mind, a witch can go by more than just one. You grew up out here and know as well as I a witch is not always who they seem."

"Well, there won't be many like this one. His name is John Etcitty, and it is said he eats little children for his dinner." Both men smiled at this, as every naughty little child thereabouts, has at one time or another, been threatened with being eaten by a witch, should they not straighten up and try to do better.

Harley grew more serious. "John Etcitty is the person I'm looking for all right. Even if he hasn't eaten any children, I suspect he has done things just as bad."

"What do you know he's done...for certain? Has he harmed anyone you know?" The old man's voice had changed, grown a little more distant, with a sharper edge. Eldon tapped his fingers on the table for a few seconds, then seeming to collect himself, began speaking in a more amiable tone. Once again becoming the old man Harley had known for so much of his life. "Do you even know what this man looks like, Harley?" he asked shaking his head.

"I have only seen glimpses of him, and then only at a distance." Thinking on it, Harley was forced to consider the man who took a shot at Sam might not have been John Etcitty at all.

Eldon Bitsui shook his head, letting go a breath in a gentle sigh, appearing almost relieved to hear this. He then leaned in a little closer. "Tell me what it is that happened, and if you are sure this John Etcitty is the one you are looking for. If he is, then I will help you find him.

Over the next few minutes Harley recounted the sad story of young Sam Klah and how someone tried to kill the boy twice in as many days, without any perceivable reason. He related the wild chase across that desolate rimrock country to the west—confiding how close he himself had come to being a victim.

Their conversation was interrupted by the sound of wood being split with an axe, and Harley knew Thomas Begay had taken it upon himself to make firewood for the *hogan*. It was a chore that would have come as readily to the man as taking a breath. He and Eldon sat listening a few minutes longer, silently gauging the strokes, and judging the power behind them, all without saying a word.

Finally, Harley spoke the obvious, a trait he was known for, "It seems Thomas has decided to make himself useful; he must have taken a liking to you—he doesn't always do the right thing."

When the door was thrown open, a rush of cool air blew into the *hogan*. Harley, assuming it was Thomas was surprised to see a woman, with an armload of kindling, edging her way in. Trying to steady the wood with both hands, she pushed the door shut with her foot, and stared at Harley a moment, wondering who he was.

Still glancing at him on her way to the wood box, she dumped the splintered cedar into an old metal coal bucket beside the stove. Never once did she take her eyes off the man across from her father. She turned to Eldon, saying, "There's a man out there chopping up our wood." She was a small woman, pleasant enough to look at, almost pretty, should one ignore the state of her outer wear. She was splattered with mud from top to bottom—her hair awry, it too, spattered in such a way some might find it comical.

Her father frowned. "Did the sheep push you into the watering hole again Daughter? That hasn't happened in a long time."

The woman frowned in her defense. "Those three mules came running up to the fence, spooking the sheep, and knocked me right over in the mud." The woman looked down at herself for the first time and then, glancing over at Harley, a delicate shudder shook her shoulders. Pushing a tangled whisp of wet hair back from her forehead, she held her hands palms up in a helpless gesture of defeat.

Harley, not knowing what else to do, stared back, unable to think of any words that might help.

The old man considered the pair for a moment as another thought came to him. "Celia, take some clean clothes out to the summer *hogan* and clean up. I will get started on supper until you get back."

Without another word, his daughter went to a chest at the rear of the room, gathered a small bundle, and left for the brush arbor. When she was out of hearing, the old man apologized, saying, "The girl ordinarily makes a better appearance than this, Harley. It's just that she doesn't know much about mules and didn't expect... well, you'll see." He got up from his chair, with a knowing smile, and went to the stove.

Rather than sitting there looking like a fool, Harley followed behind him, kneeling to lay a bed of kindling in the firebox, and topping it with the last remaining chunks of wood. No sooner had he touched a match to the tinder, the door opened once again and he turned to see Thomas Begay pushed his way into the room, carrying an armload of split cedar.

"There's more, but this should be enough to get you started." Putting the cedar chunks in the wood-box Thomas, looking around for the woman, said, "I saw the whole thing but couldn't get over there in time to do anything about it." Thomas started a smile but changed expression when he saw the frown on Harley's face. "I should have let her know those mules haven't been around any sheep, to speak of. It takes 'em a while to get used to those woolies, you know."

Harley was embarrassed by his thoughtless mules and his face grew red at the thought of the woman's embarrassment on their account.

The old man waved it away, saying, "I've seen many a sheep stomped into the ground by a mule. Horses don't seem to mind them that much, but a mule will take offense the first time or two he runs into them."

Then turning to Thomas, he asked, "Are the sheep up in the corrals now?"

"They are all locked up, I checked 'em myself. They'll be fine now. Your dogs were as surprised as I was."

The old man shook his head. "Those dogs are young and have never been around mules either. They'll know to watch 'em next time." He threw Thomas a glance. "There's a sack of potatoes in that cupboard over there if you'd like to slice some up, and some onions too."

Harley rose from the stove. "I'll do the onions."

When Celia Bitsui came in from the ramada, she looked quite a different person. Her hair, wet from a quick wash, was slicked back in a neatly styled bun, and she wore a new dress under a spotless apron. She was indeed a pretty woman and now, with a new aura of confidence about her, she asserted herself by shooing her father from the stove and took charge of the mutton, just now starting to sizzle in an iron skillet. Smiling at Harley Ponyboy, she motioned him away as well. "You men are lucky we butchered a ewe yesterday, otherwise this would be Spam in this skillet."

Thomas, never shy around women, laughingly proclaimed, "Spam is probably what we'd be grilling around a campfire right now, if Eldon hadn't invited us to supper." Then he quickly added, with an approving glance, "You folks are lucky to have good water right here by the house. It was a long time before we got a well put in, and the water is not all that great."

The men reseated themselves around the table and watched as Celia busied herself about the stove. They were hungry, and it smelled good. Their coffee cups were still on the table, and the woman took time to bring the pot over for a refill.

Harley, watching her at the stove, became achingly aware of what he'd been missing these past years. Not just the cooking, but how much he'd missed having someone around in the evening to talk to—though he'd not got up the courage to do much of that yet. Granted, neither of the past women he'd been involved with had been much at cooking. Nor, when it came right down to it, were either of them particularly pleasant companions. This woman seemed to a have a better disposition. Not that he had any real thought of pursuing the matter. She might even have a husband somewhere, for all he knew.

When Celia brought plates of food and a loaf of white bread to the table, the men were quick to make room for her, and the four of them quickly began to eat, paying their full attention to the food, in the manner of any hardworking people.

When things slowed down, the woman looked over at Harley and asked if he needed more of anything. He shook his head and seemed unable to come up with anything which might further the conversation. After taking a sip of coffee, the woman turned to her father as though something had suddenly come to mind.

"I saw that man again today. High up...leaning against that lightning struck pine at the top. Just watching. That's the second time this week. Both times when I was on my way down and had the sheep on the second bench from the top. There is only one place on the rim you can see from there. I don't know what he wants, coming around here like that, but it makes me nervous."

Thomas shot Harley a guarded glance. Harley, his mouth full and chewing contentedly, hadn't seemed to notice. But he had noticed the frown that flashed across the old man's face. Yet gave no indication of it.

The woman, taking her cue from the old man, said no more about it. Nor did anyone else.

After dinner, Celia began clearing the table and, though the woman protested, Harley Ponyboy jumped up and lent a hand. Relenting, with a half-smile Celia started the dishes.

Thomas and Eldon stayed at the table, pouring themselves more coffee as they talked about sheep and other things of a like nature.

The two at the wash buckets spoke quietly between themselves. Harley, slowly regaining some modicum of courage, became more animated when he told her about his son and their place in Waterflow. Celia listened with interest, obviously taken with his more urban lifestyle. It wasn't hard to see it would be more to her liking than this isolated land of few people.

~~~~~

That night, rolled in their blankets on opposite sides of the narrow brush shelter, Thomas turned to peer through the darkness at the shadowy form on the other side and could no longer hold his tongue. "When you and the old man were alone this evening, did he say anything about the man we were looking for?" The tall man pushed himself up on a bony elbow. "You did ask him...right?"

"I asked him."

Thomas waited a few moments, thinking Harley was just groggy with sleep and might have more to say. After waiting a few minutes and hearing nothing further, he frowned into the dark and said, "If you don't want to talk about it, just say so. This is your party, I'm just along for the ride. But as far as I'm concerned, both of those people know more than they're letting on. I know Eldon is your friend, but I think he's holding back."

A heavy sigh came from the other side of the shelter. "Yes, he is. Eldon didn't want to talk about it. But I think you're right, he's covering for someone."

Thomas heard him turn away and, in only a few minutes, there came the muffled sound of snoring. He took this to mean the man said all he was going to say and was through talking.

I have known Harley a long time, and he's smarter than most give him credit for, He's not going to leave it at this... Not a Chance.

~~~~~~

It was two hours before daylight when Thomas Begay stirred in his blankets and raised his head to see his friend Harley already up and putting on his coat. They were at a good altitude here—the night colder than it should have been, given the time of year. He could see his breath in the frosty air and struggled to see the time on his plastic Timex. Muttering under his breath he finally managed, "A little early, isn't it? It won't be light enough to see for a while yet. "

Harley edged closer and nudged him with the toe of a boot. "Up." He said, then moving to the makeshift washstand with its bucket of icy water, he splashed his face vigorously face a couple of times, then shivered, despite the heavy coat. "There's a good slice of moon this morning, enough to make our way to the rim. By time we get up there there'll be light enough to read sign."

Thomas groaned as he rose, shaking his head to clear the cobwebs, then pulled on his clothes, cast a dour look through the brushy roof of the ramada to gauge the stars. Even with his wristwatch, he still double-checked time by the stars. "No coffee this morning?"

"Not just yet. There is something I want to see before the sun dries things out up there. We have food in our saddle bags...at least, I do."

Thomas nodded wearily, taking his turn at the bucket before drying his face on his sleeve and pulling on his boots. Each man took a blanket, rolled in their slickers, and Thomas planned on taking his saddle gun as well.

The two gave the *hogan* a wide berth as they moved quietly down to the corrals. Both the old man's dogs were watching somewhat expectantly as they lifted their noses to catch the men's scent, neither offered more than a low growl deep in their throats.

As they put distance between them and the *hogan,* Thomas whispered, "You're thinking of the man the woman saw up on the rim?"

"If it was a man."

Thomas blanched noticeably, even in the scant light of the moon. Though he hadn't let himself dwell on it, he knew exactly what Harley was talking about. If the rumors were true, and John Etcitty was a witch, that could have been almost anything up on the rim. Maybe a Skinwalker, sent to stand watch and report back. *That's why Harley wanted to check for sign, while the ground was fresh with frost. Even a Yeenaaldiooshii might leave some hint of his passage in those conditions, should a man know what to look for.*

Leaving Harley at the horse trailer to ready their gear, Thomas went to catch up their mounts. He chose the best two of his mules, leaving the horse and a pack mule in the pasture. There was no question these mules would make a better job of the rough and dangerous work ahead. The moon, slim though it was, would likely be down before daylight, leaving them in the dark and on the worst of the upper trail. It wasn't far distance-wise, but it was a steep climb and would be slow going.

As the pair rode to the head of the canyon, steep walls shaded what little moon there was. It fell to the mules' instinctive caution to find their way, with the riders giving them their heads, and leaving the animals to navigate the trail as they saw fit.

Herding sheep for Eldon as a teenager, Harley Ponyboy was fairly certain he knew the spot Celia Bitsui saw the mysterious stranger. There were three, long flat benches on the way to the top, and she'd said he was at the one place visible from the second bench. A lightning struck pine should not be hard to locate.

A dim glow was beginning to outline the edges of the canyon wall as Thomas, bringing up the rear on the slower of the two animals, felt the mule stumble on a loose rock. He instantly lifted the reins, setting himself back in the saddle as the animal scrambled to regain his footing. The softer sandstone edge of the trail had crumbled sending debris hurtling into the darkness. The man listened a long moment, finally hearing a faint crash a hundred or more feet below. The mule calmly continued on his way, as though the incident was common enough and all in a day's work.

Though Harley Ponyboy was well in advance of the laggards, he heard the mishap that might have proven disastrous for the average horse yet paid it no mind in the case of the surefooted mule. While he was anxious to top out the rim and focused on what manner of thing they might be stalking, Eldon Bitsui's daughter still lingered in the back of his mind. While he had mixed feelings about Celia, he still could not help being curious. On the one hand, his past judgment had been poor when it came to women, yet he couldn't deny his attraction to the woman. Surely a grown man couldn't be afflicted in the manner teenagers such as Sam Klah and Ida Marie Begay were smitten? The idea of it brought a smile to his face.

Pausing his long-eared mount, Harley turned in the saddle to listen for his friend's mule. Though dawn was near, he was still having a hard time picking out the lightning tree. It might be a while yet. *Thomas has the sharper eye. I'll wait here a bit. The two of us will find it soon enough.* Stepping off the mule, he looked for a place to tie up. It had been a hard pull to the top, even now the mule was breathing hard. Not winded, or lathered up, yet his neck was slick with sweat despite the cold air. He would wait a few minutes for him to cool out before pulling the saddle—being sure to tie him high enough he couldn't roll, which a mule is likely to do.

As he was loosening his cinch, Harley could hear a mule laboring up the last steep bit at the rim. By the time Thomas tied up, Harley had dug out a couple of sticks of convenience-store jerky, and some little individually wrapped slices of fruit cake—a treat he had long favored.

Thomas took his share of the meager breakfast with a grimace. "You know I don't like these little fruitcakes, Harley. After all these years I'd have thought you might have a little more consideration."

Harley chuckled, saying, "Well, I *do* like 'em. You don't have to eat these things if you don't like 'em. I wouldn't force a man into eating something he don't like."

Thomas snorted, peeling the plastic wrap off the sticky little cake, he stuffed nearly half in his mouth. Then, with a disgusted look, turned and offered the other half to his mule, who barely sniffed the treat before daintily working his lips around it chewing along with his rider. The sun was now edging over the ridge behind them as Harley cast about for the marker the woman mentioned. Being careful where he stepped, he leaned down to inspect the state of the red soil. Judging the night's frost to be near perfect, he nodded his approval to Thomas who was sucking the remnants of fruit cake out his teeth. His mule, head raised and lips drawn back in a grin, appeared to be doing the same.

In the first weak light of day, it took no more than a few minutes to locate the charred tree. Raising a cautionary hand to his friend, Harley approached the tree at an angle, taking advantage of the oblique rays of light to define the slightest outline. After only a few feet he paused to motion Thomas forward. Now speechless, Harley could only point to the base of the tree. A woman, throwing off her blankets, rose stiff and shivering from her hours of waiting.

Celia Bitsui held up her hands, as though to block their way. "My father woke in the night, suspecting you might do this. He sent me to give you a final warning. Do not follow after this person. He is *Yeenaaldiooshii* and evil beyond imagining."

Looking about, Harley noticed the ground around the base of the tree, had been swept clean with pine boughs.

The woman spoke again, and so forcefully the men were obliged to listen. "My father says the person you are looking for is not up here. He says to come back down. We will eat and talk more about who you should really be looking for." Saying this, she took up her blankets and started down the trail—only to turn with a final admonishment, "You are putting yourself in danger up here. I promise, you will learn more down there, than you will up here."

Thomas and Harley stood looking after her, their faces a study in contradiction. Returning to their animals, Thomas mounted then looking over at his friend, said, "I'll follow her down to make sure she's safe. You might want to cut a wide circle up here to see what you can find." He shook his head toward their backtrail. "This woman came to warn someone alright, but not us." With a wave he called back over his shoulder, "I'll be back as quick as I can."

Harley Ponyboy was already in the saddle, heading back to the lightning tree.

Chapter 17

Survival

Returning home from work, Charlie Yazzie was surprised to find Harley had dropped off his son at their place...possibly for a few days. He didn't mind Sue keeping the boy, she was growing more attached to the child every day. And, with the help of their own two children, he knew little Harley wouldn't be much trouble. What did bother him, was Harley and Thomas taking off like a couple of vigilantes without any warning. He knew exactly what they were up to.

Charlie had a pretty good idea where they were going, too, and knew it could be dangerous. Their last run-in with Sam's assailant should have been warning enough. It was likely Harley was still brooding over the rattlesnake incident that, coupled with his twice failed attempt to corner the man, would be working on his head. Charlie figured it would be only a matter of time before he decided to do something about it, but had advised him to hold off, pending his investigation. Apparently, the advice had fallen on deaf ears. Thomas Begay would have been in complete agreement with his old friend. The two were of a like mind in most things—and neither were much on waiting, for anything.

Calling Lucy Tallwoman, Thomas's wife said she had been in town on Council business and, unfortunately, had not been there to argue them out of the notion. Lucy went on to say she was certain the pair were most likely headed to Monument Valley, where they had been so humiliated by the would-be assassin's escape.

For Charlie this only verified the two were determined to take matters into their own hands. Not that they didn't have a long history of mixing in the affairs of both he, and Billy Red Clay. Granted, there'd been a few times he'd been happy to see them jump in when he was in a tough spot, but this was an entirely different matter. He was convinced now that he and Billy were on the verge of uncovering something big enough that he couldn't afford to have these two interfere—not when he was this close. Charlie felt Erwin Johnson's growing paper trail of investment scams alone should be strong enough to prosecute the man on any number of charges, despite many being beyond the statute of limitations, but it would only take one to put him away for a very long time. Then too, there was Billy Red Clay's ongoing investigation showing possible ties to the assaults on Sam Klah. *No, it shouldn't be long before we have enough to bring charges against Erwin Johnson, if Harley and Thomas don't manage to screw things up.* So far, Johnson seemed unaware he was being investigated. That was their advantage.

The Investigator thought it best he check in with Billy Red Clay and punched in the man's extension wondering if the Navajo Policeman knew his Uncle was stirring things up again.

"Billy... uh, Yes, I know they did... No. Only what Lucy told me... She called you too, huh?" Charlie listened another minute or two and, when Billy finished his rant, said, "Right, I'll meet you there in thirty minutes."

Billy Red Clay grew more disgusted with his uncle as he drove the short distance to the *Diné Bikeyah Cafe*. He had to smile at the chewing-out Thomas would likely get. Billy had clearly had it with his Uncle and was not a man to back away from a confrontation, even with those of his own clan.

Charlie was first to arrive at the restaurant, taking a window seat near the back, keeping an eye on the parking lot as he signaled the waitress there would be two. The place was nearly empty, unusual for this early in the day. Several things were always on the bill of fare, regardless of what time it was, or which menu was featured. The Investigator already knew what he wanted.

Looking out the window, he saw Billy Red Clay pulling in next to Charlie's Tribal unit, right on time. The Officer came to a stop in a cloud of dust. The wind was picking up out of the south, pushing trash, and herding a few small dust devils across the lot. Billy got out holding to his hat with one hand. Spotting Charlie through the window, he threw him a two fingered salute as he hurried past the window and on to the front entrance.

Charlie was smiling to himself as the young Policeman pushed through the door and headed his way. Billy's uniform was impeccable as usual. Boots freshly polished and black Stetson pulled low on his forehead. *It's what a Navajo Cop should look like* Charlie thought to himself. The man was a credit to his calling.

The waitress, already on the way with a coffee pot in one hand and menus in the other. She took out her pad and stood tapping one foot in rhythm with the jukebox.

Charlie turned up his cup, and with a booted foot shoved out a seat for Billy as the Policeman took off his hat. The man considered the Stetson with a critical eye as he brushed off a spot of dust, before carefully hanging the 10x beaver on the back of a chair. Navajo men take great pride in their hats and this one cost a week's wages. Without saying anything the men waited for the waitress to pour their coffee and hand them each a menu. Charlie passed his back without looking at it.

"Cheeseburger Deluxe for me. Mayo on the side please." Pointing at Billy, he added, "Put his order on my check, if you will."

Billy surprised them both by holding up a hand to the woman and shaking his head. "Thanks Charlie, but I can't eat anything right now." The Investigator caught the look on his face and spoke softly to the waitress, "Make both of those orders to go will you, Merna. We'll pick 'em up at the counter on the way out."

As quickly as the woman left, Billy's face dropped and he breathed a ragged sigh. "I've got some bad news, Charlie." He glanced out the window, frowning at the weather a moment before reluctantly turning back to the table. "Agent Smith called, just as I was leaving the office." Billy hesitated a moment as though wondering the best way to put it, apparently deciding there wasn't any good way, just gave to him straight. "Norman Klee is dead."

The Investigator, a blank look on his face, coffee cup half-way to his lips, had to make a conscious effort to get the words out. "What happened, Billy?"

"Not sure yet. He was found a couple-miles from his house, out on the old roller dam road. Dead at the wheel of his truck." The young Cop looked away as he went on. "There was a vacuum cleaner hose from the tail pipe through the back slider. The engine had run out of fuel...but not before it killed him."

"Who called it in?"

"They don't know who called it in, but whoever it was called the FBI first. Kind of unusual don't you think? It was right here on the reservation, where the average person would have called Tribal Police first...wouldn't you say, Charlie?"

The Investigator bit his lip. "Dammit! That old man never harmed a single soul, that I know of." A vague realization was forming in the back of his mind; that this old man's death might be his fault.

"Oh God," he whispered, catching his breath. "You don't suppose someone found out he was talking to me...do you?"

Billy looked down without answering. He'd looked up to Charlie since he was a boy. The man's unflinching dedication to the job, and his reputation for honesty and integrity, had long been a benchmark for the young Officer.

Billy was troubled now by the look he saw in the man's eyes—a look he wouldn't soon forget.

Charlie sat his cup down, staring at it for nearly a minute before lifting his head.

"Autopsy?" he asked.

"The FBI pulled out all the stops. They have people on that right now."

"So, do they think it's a suicide? I mean, that would make sense I suppose. Norman must have had a lot of pressure on him, what with this business with Erwin Johnson. Norman had to know there was some kind of legal action coming and, that he most likely would be called as a witness."

"It's too early to call it a suicide, Charlie, if that's what you're thinking. Fred wouldn't make that determination this early in the investigation. The old man had quite a welt on his forehead...didn't break the skin. Maybe he just hit his head on the wheel when he passed out. No one can say for sure at this point."

Charlie shook his head. "I just talked to the man yesterday. He seemed in good enough spirits—certainly didn't show any sign he might be contemplating anything like this. But I can't believe it was some spur of the moment thing either. I have to think there's more to it than suicide. Even knowing the man for so short a time, Norman Klee was not the sort of person I would expect to do something like this." He passed a hand in front of his face. "Does his wife know?

"Yes, she does. From what I gather, she's taking it pretty hard. Officer Ben Nez is still out there with her, He's Cedar Clan, like her."

Charlie raised his eyes in thought. "As far as I know, the woman doesn't really have anyone but Norman. They didn't have much money either, from what I gathered. I'm not sure what she'll do now. Dammit. I just can't believe Norman would purposely leave her in such a situation."

Billy thought about this, wondering if Charlie could be right. The FBI's official position was as yet undetermined, as would be expected at this stage of an investigation, he'd had the feeling Agent Smith himself was somewhat puzzled by the case. "There's some of the women coming out to stay with Mrs. Klee when Officer Nez leaves." Billy then took this opportunity to expand on what he'd already reported. "So, what with the woman carrying on and all, Ben didn't get a chance to question her before the FBI got there. Of course, those Agents couldn't understand much of what she was saying, anyway. My guess is, she was probably talking Old Navajo a lot of the time." He grimaced. "I'm thinkin' them white boys won't get much out of her."

"No, I guess not. I expect I'd better give Fred's people time to finish up out there, then pay the poor woman a visit. I'd like to express my condolences and have a word with her, if she's up to it."

As the two grew silent, taking turns staring out the window, watching the first raindrops slide down the glass, each wondering how this tragedy might ultimately affect their investigation.

The sky turned darker as the wind strengthened, sucking up sand from the parking lot to pepper the window glass. "Looks like a storm blowing in," Charlie said quietly. Then, shoving back his chair, he noticed Merna standing at the front register, holding up their orders with an expectant gaze. Turning to the Navajo Cop, Charlie murmured, "Life can sometimes be a real bitch, huh Billy?"

Chapter 18

No Rainbow

The frontal system rolled in fast and dirty, then after little more than an hour, blew itself out the same way. No rain, no rainbow.

Charlie Yazzie went alone to see Imogene Klee. He felt that, because Norman worked for him, it was his place to go. The mobile home was at the edge of town, not all that far from where Norman was found dead. The front yard had not a single car in it. Apparently, Officer Ben Nez and the Bureau Agents had finished their business and left. The woman would now be waiting for her clan sisters, who would be bringing food, and that would take time.

Charlie pulled up in front, wondering what he could possibly say to this woman that might be of the slightest help. During his years with Legal Services, he had often been charged with this duty. Seldom did he go away feeling he'd left the bereaved any better off. In this case, however, the visit was two-fold. In addition to any comfort he might offer, there were questions posed by the manner in which her husband had died.

Charlie's Navajo was not perfect, but good enough, and he'd often found such people actually spoke better English than they let on to whites. It was possible the woman could have valuable input regarding Norman's state of mind in the hours prior. This was important to Charlie.

Imogene Klee answered the door by the second knock, eyes red from crying, perhaps expecting it might be her clan sisters, and causing her to put on her best face.

The Investigator, hat in hand, introduced himself as Norman's boss, offering his sincerest condolences, then asked Imogene if he might have a moment of her time.

The woman appeared confused at this, but opened the door wide to invite him in. The newer double-wide was roomy, clean, and well furnished. As he was being offered a chair in the living room, the Investigator noticed the generous bookshelves flanking a small desk.

"Norman spoke well of you, Mr. Yazzie." The woman said this in English, but clearly wasn't comfortable in the language. She asked, "Would you like something to drink? I still have coffee left over from those others that were here this morning. I could get you a cup."

"No, I'm pretty well coffee'd out right now, Mrs. Klee." Charlie was sure she was feeling the same at this point. She would not have failed to offer everyone coffee this morning, with at least some pretense of taking part. "I'll try to take as little of your time as possible, I know others will be along soon. I was wondering if you could tell me what frame of mind your husband was in when he left home this morning? What he might have said, if you can recall?"

The woman shuddered through a deep breath, then considered Charlie a moment longer before answering. "Norman seemed a little nervous, you know. He'd had a call early this morning that upset him. He was in here having his coffee... I was still in the bed...I haven't felt well for some time now. Norman would say I should sleep in—he makes his own breakfast these days." She paused to reflect. "The telephone woke me when it rang."

"Do you happen to know who it was, or what was said?"

"Well, I don't know who it was, but after I came fully awake, I could hear Norman talking a little. Not all of it you know, but some. He sounded a little angry...it was about money, from what I could tell."

Charlie looked up at this. "I see. Has Norman been worried about money lately?"

"We never talk very much about money, Mr. Yazzie. Norman said that was his job and I shouldn't have to worry about it." Imogene paused momentarily, appearing to think back on what she knew of their finances. "I don't believe money was a problem, not for a long while now. Norman went to Farmington a year or so ago and bought us this trailer house. It was almost new, as you can see. We don't have any payments on it that I know of. Norman must have saved the money to buy it. He was good at saving money. He was an accountant you know. It's what he went to college for."

Charlie tried not to show his surprise at so sizeable an outright purchase. He had assumed they were renting, like most in the area.

"Norman only worked a few days a week, isn't that right, Mrs. Klee?"

"That's so, but he did some work on his days off, too. He told me there was a couple people in his office who worked on the side, just like him. He told me that several times. I told him I thought he might be overdoing it, but he would just laugh it off." She teared up at this. "He never wanted me to worry about him."

Charlie glanced over at the bookcase, where the desk with file drawers down one side, had a number of folders stacked on top. Turning back to the woman, he answered, "Yes, several of our people apparently take work home with them. We get pretty busy from time to time. I suppose it's the only way they can keep up."

The Investigator was thinking of Isabell Joe's husband, William, who he'd already connected to Erwin Johnson's operation. William Joe was also dead, and he made a mental note to further investigate that, as well.

Uncertain what to think of this latest development, Charlie became even more confused... *What was Norman Klee's part in this thing?* Whatever it was, it didn't sound good for the man, no matter how he sliced it.

The sound of vehicles arriving interrupted their conversation, the pair turning toward the door as they listened to car doors closing, then heard voices outside.

Imogene went to the window and, with a sad little smile, waved at the women gathering in the yard. Turning back to Charlie, she murmured, "It's some of the ladies from my clan," and quickly moved to open the door.

Charlie rose to make his goodbyes, standing aside for the women as he watched them file in with solemn faces and covered dishes. Several of the women he recognized, though he couldn't place them all right off.

~~~~~

Later, on his way back to work Charlie, couldn't help a rush of disappointment in his late employee. What he'd learned at the Klee place was totally unexpected. He had not thought it of the unassuming little man. Still, it was not enough to make a case either way. Was it suicide, or was it murder? In his view, either was still a possibility. At any rate he would let Billy Red Clay know, and he could be the one to pass his suspicions along to Fred Smith at the Bureau. As Tribal Liaison Officer, it was general procedure that Legal Services should go through Billy Red Clay in these matters. A procedure not always followed in the past, but it was how the system was designed to work. Both agencies had recently agreed to adhere more closely to this protocol, and he figured this as good a time as any to begin implementing it to a stricter degree. Turning up the volume on the two-way, he picked up the mic and called in, only to hear Arlene on the speaker. "Uh... Arlene... where's the girl who usually handles the radio?"

"She's not here Mr. Yazzie. She's born to the Cedar Clan, so she had to go over to Norman Klee's place to be with his wife." *Well, that places one of the women I saw there.* There was a notable chill in the receptionist's voice, and it occurred to Charlie she'd already heard of Norman Klee's death—most likely by way of the office communication's operator. Arlene thought a lot of Norman, and this was going to take some explaining, once he took time to explain it to himself.

The Investigator was no more back in his office than Arlene signaled there was a call from the Bureau.

Senior Agent Fred Smith came on the line, with a gruffer tone than Charlie was used to hearing from the man. "Billy Red Clay called to pass along the substance of your visit to Norman Klee's wife, and seemed under the impression you think Klee's death might be a homicide?"

"I've been leaning that way, yes." Charlie wasn't easily cowed, even by the FBI. Agent Smith was an old friend, but this was business.

After a short pause, the Senior Agent moderated his tone a bit, saying, "I've just read my people's report from *their* time out at the Klee place. You might be surprised to learn, the exhaust hose used to asphyxiate Mr. Klee, came from his own home. His wife stated he'd taken it to town to have a new end put on it." Fred went silent, waiting to see what the Investigator thought of this information.

Charlie, unprepared though he was, didn't stutter when he said, "I didn't know that Fred, but it really doesn't change things, does it? Unless you have something else, I'm unaware of, homicide still can't be ruled out. That hose may have been an accessory of convenience rather than an instrument of choice. It would have served the purpose equally well, don't you think?" Charlie then moderated his own tone, saying, "Admittedly, I'm not as sure as I was before, but the possibility does still exist."

Fred chuckled, "Charlie, I was pretty sure the lawyer in you would see it this way, and you're right, too. I was just yanking your chain. At this point there's a lot more we need to know about what happened out there. Beyond what I've already said, I don't know any more than you do." The Agent sounded even more conciliatory when he said. "What say you drop by the office in a couple of hours? The autopsy report should be in by then, and you and I, and Billy, can go over it together. Maybe that will give us a little more to base these suspicions on."

Charlie mulled it over and, sensing the prospect of some sort of resolution, agreed to the meeting. Hanging up the phone, he heard a soft knock and as the door opened, he looked up to see the grim visage of his receptionist. Motioning her into the office, he was struck by the obvious animosity in her greeting.

"Mr. Yazzie," She said, flatly.

This was the second time today she'd addressed him as 'Mr. Yazzie', *the woman should have been down to 'Boss' by now.*

"Your wife called to ask if you would stop at the store on your way home. Little Harley is drinking them out of milk and she thought you should pick up another gallon." The receptionist had the morning reports in her hand, and without another word plopped them on the desk, then flounced out of the office not even closing the door behind her.

Charlie watched her go with a frown, he definitely needed to have a talk with the woman, and before the end of the day if possible.

Two hours later, the Investigator pulled up at the Federal building and parked next to Billy Red Clay's Tribal unit. Getting out, he reached over and put his hand on the hood—stone cold. *Billy has been here a while.* Taking the steps to the Federal building two at a time, he was huffing by the time he reached the second floor. The secretary waved him through to the Agent's office—she'd known Charlie a long time and was forewarned he was on his way.

Opening the big mahogany door, Charlie was amused to see Billy Red Clay sitting in Fred's posh leather chair, spinning it back and forth in a half-circle. The Navajo Cop jumped up as the Investigator came in.

"Where's Fred?" The Investigator smiled.

"He's down the hall...bathroom." Billy's face took on another shade of red as he shrugged and smiled back.

"Trying his chair on for size, huh?"

"Well, you know..."

Both men grinned.

"Don't let him catch you at that. He's particular who sits in his chair." Charlie made a gun of his thumb and forefinger and clicked it at him. "Did the Autopsy report on Norman Klee come in?"

"No. Not as yet... Fred said it's on its way down from County, should be here in a few minutes, he thinks."

The two men were standing by the window chatting, when the Senior Agent finally came back into the room, carrying a packet.

"Good to see you two gentlemen again." Fred looked first at Charlie. "How's the family?"

"Oh, good...good as can be expected. Sue's taking care of Harley's son the next day or so."

Fred was a family man himself and nodded his head to let the Investigator know he got it. He had a large brown envelope under one arm and settled in behind his desk as he began opening the autopsy packet. Stopping suddenly, Fred frowned at his name plate. He reached out and turned it to face forward, then went back to opening the envelope. The metal clasp was caught, and it took him a moment of concerted effort to free it.

Charlie looked over at Billy with a hint of a smile and a raised eyebrow. The young officer seemed engrossed in adjusting the cuff of his shirt and appeared not to notice.

Looking up, Fred gazed at the two men a moment... "This, as you might guess, is the Autopsy report on Mr. Klee. Hot off the press, as it were." Fred pulled out the packet and spread the papers on his desk. "There will be a copy for each of you at the end of the meeting. I'll try to just hit the high spots for you right now, but you might want to go over it later at your discretion, should you get a chance."

Taking up a sheet of diagrams, he scanned it briefly before passing it around. The second sheet, one of several, described the autopsy process in minute detail, some of which Fred seemed to skip over as he explained the base procedure to the two Navajo lawmen. Billy squirmed in his seat, losing a shade or two of his ruddy complexion. It was the Policeman's first time hearing the nuts and bolts of the clinical process.

Fred was quick to point out that the mark on Norman's forehead had been deemed, almost certainly, to have been caused by his head hitting the steering wheel. "That was," he said, "the official determination."

Glancing at the report, Charlie asked if the mark had been inflicted before or after the man's death, or if decerning that was even a possibility.

The Agent fingered through the papers, pulling one out and studying it a moment before saying, "It appears the injury was inflicted so close to the clinical time of death it could not be decerned with any degree of accuracy.

Billy Red Clay, now looking slightly askance at the Investigator thought, *surely, Charlie's through running this around in a circle now.* What the young Policeman actually said, though, was, "Well, I would guess this leaves us right back where we started."

Fred, holding up the last sheet of the report, shook his head. "You don't know the half of it, Billy. I've saved the best for last. This is the verdict on the actual cause of death. As it turns out, Norman Klee died of a massive heart attack. He was dead before he had time to be asphyxiated."

The three lawmen sat looking at one another as though they hadn't fully understood the report. Surely there was something, somewhere, in those papers which could point a finger in some more definitive direction?

Chapter 19

The Anomaly

It was full daylight before Thomas Begay followed Eldon Bitsui's daughter far enough down the trail to be assured the woman would make it safely on to her camp. There had been little doubt in his mind she would be fine, but now no one could blame them for any mishap that might befall the woman. In any case, it would take Harley some time to sort out a trail up on top.

He didn't push the mule as hard this second time to the top. The animal seemed the better for it. When he reached the lightning tree, he was expecting to run across Harley close to where he'd left him. He would leave him a good trail regardless—of that he was certain. After their experience of the week before, he hoped his friend might be a little more cautious this time. Harley's sprained ankle, from their last little adventure, had barely healed to the point he was able to walk without a limp.

At the top, Thomas let the mule rest for a short time then cut his own circle, searching closer in than Harley would have, yet sure to cross the tracker's sign at some point. He was nearly half-way around his planned route, only four or five miles from the rim as the crow flies.

The first sign appeared without warning. The tall Navajo leaned over to gaze at the prints for several minutes. Somewhat taken aback, he searched the terrain around him. *These are the tracks of Harley's mule alright, but it seems to be meandering around grazing, not going in any particular direction.* The thing that concerned him most, were the hoofprints themselves. They weren't deep enough to indicate the animal carried a rider, and there were no man tracks either, so Harley hadn't just dismounted to lead the animal. No, the mule making these tracks was all by itself, as far as he could see.

Thomas got down from his own animal and examined the prints more carefully. Though none of Harley's mules were in the least herd-bound and would go off alone in any direction they were pointed, this mule was wanting some company. Despite any training to the contrary, the mule is, by nature, a herd animal and will eventually seek the company of other equines. As Thomas stood pondering this development, his mount put his nose in the wind and gave a loud bray. Sensing his pal was somewhere nearby, this mule seemed determined to locate him. In only a minute, there came a reply from downwind, and Thomas guessed it to be no more than a quarter mile away, knowing full well sound was a tricky thing in these canyons.

One thing was easy to figure, Harley would be somewhere ahead of him now, and on foot. His mule, now that it had located this one, would be headed this way. It would be foolish to do other than wait. In the meantime, Thomas fished out a stick of jerky, gnawing at the dried meat as he searched out the surrounding country. Old growth spruce, of a good size, separated grassy parks running to the top of the ridge. Hearing the trickle of hidden water, he looked about for the source. He wanted a drink, and so did the mule. That was the beauty of these high rims. There was plenty of water if a man knew where to find it. It wasn't always that way down below.

Mountain springs often cut so narrow and deep a ditch the water itself couldn't be seen until nearly on top of them. Leading the mule, he moved in the most likely direction, finally locating a small but swift moving trickle of snowmelt, no more than fifty feet away. Not being familiar with this particular mule, he couldn't be sure it wouldn't take a mind to pull loose and go looking for his friend. The icy water was down deep enough that Thomas had to retrieve his drinking cup from a saddle bag to have any hope of reaching it.

His mule, down on one knee, poked his long nose far enough below the bank to drink, then rose, and stretching his neck, let out another ear-splitting bray. This was soon answered by a more distant bray and within minutes a clatter of hooves headed their way. Thomas's mule skittered sideways in the direction of the animal, shaking his head as though considering he might meet him half-way.

Thomas saw the mule coming on a high lope. It's head twisted to one side to clear the dragging reins—stirrups flopping against its ribs at every jump. The animal, already in a lather, brayed at the sight of them.

There was no Harley Ponyboy.

As quick as he spotted them, the approaching animal put on the brakes, slowing to a trot, then stopping altogether to touch noses with his tethered friend. Thomas, catching up the new-comer's reins, had to admit a common horse would probably have stepped on those reins, either taking a tumble, or tearing them loose from the bridle. *These long-ears have their good points, and that's a fact.*

Examining Harley's saddle, Thomas was quick to note scuffs on the cantle, and on one skirt. Twigs and leaves were caught in the flaps of the saddlebags. This mule had bolted from something, likely tearing through a good patch of brush, at some point—probably after parting company with his rider. The lanky *Diné* turned to his own mule and leaned across the saddle a moment to consider what might have happened. Reaching into a saddlebag he pulled out a packet of soda crackers and, as though one in a trance, began to eat. He couldn't figure what had happened to his friend. He'd never seen the mule that could throw Harley Ponyboy. True, the man was a little past his prime. But not that far past.

A towering bank of black clouds were building to the northwest, the sort that might bring big rain. Thomas watched a few minutes trying to decide if the storm would miss him or not, probably not he guessed, as he watched barbs of lightning playing along the base of the thunderheads. Whatever he was going to do he had better get at it. The last thing he wanted was to spend a night under a spruce tree in a driving rain. It was already well past noon and he calculated the storm could be on him within the next hour or two. A storm this size would likely wash out every track in the area within minutes.

He mounted up and started his backtrack of Harley's mule. He wasn't the tracker Harley Ponyboy was, but could do a workman like job, should the rain hold off. Finding where his friend came undone from his mule, might lead to some answers.

~~~~~

Harley Ponyboy took his time searching out the trail that someone had taken great pains to conceal. The effort slowed him considerably. Whoever he was following knew this rough country as well as he did and was practiced at leaving little sign of his passing. Chances were, he grew up here...just as he had.

Thomas Begay should be catching up shortly and the thought caused him to think again of the woman Celia Bitsui. *Why had her father sent her off in the night on so dangerous an errand?* He'd known this old man most of his life and never had he heard anything bad about him. *Yet Eldon clearly meant to shield this person, even knowing he'd been spying on his daughter. Why?*

He was near certain this was the same person who'd taken a shot at Sam Klah up at Doc Custer's dig. The way he stayed off the main trail, sometimes choosing long stretches through the oak brush, where the deep ground cover would hold little sign. And the way he had clearly taken his time—Harley often found places he had paused, waited for him to come within a certain distance before moving out in front again. All of his reminiscent of their previous chase.

Frequent rock outcroppings rose above the scrub oak and mountain mahogany. *Good country for an ambush, something we Diné were good at, back in the day.*

Despite his vigilance, Harley never saw the lariat loop, sailing in from behind, but he heard it, and instinctively gave his mule a good kick to the side to avoid it. But, too late. The loop settled over his shoulders, trapping his arms at his side as the mule barreled out from under him. Instantly a bellow rang out, and Harley, in midair had a glimpse of his mule turning to bolt down the trail, just before he crashed to the ground in a heap. Momentarily stunned, Harley barely felt the kick to his head, remaining oblivious to that inevitable fall into darkness.

~~~~~

Upon coming around, Harley Ponyboy's first thought was his dreams of Monster Slayer, and later White Shell Woman, which likely meant he was dead, and on his final journey to the nether world. He couldn't move his arms or legs which should have been proof enough. Yet, hearing the sound of water falling and what he took to be the far rumble of Thunderbirds, he took courage. He might not be altogether dead. Even more heartening in his befuddled state, was the sensation of freezing cold at his back, yet much warmer in front. Maybe he was only half-dead, hovering somehow between both worlds. Was it possible he might still claw his way back? So thinking, he opened one eye a crack, only enough to have a peek, maybe see which world had the stronger grip.

He found himself sitting against a rock wall, not far from a small fire smoldering in the shelter of a cave-like overhang. Bound both hand and foot, and securely tied to a large root behind him, his situation, as far as he could see, did not look good. Outside the shelter it was pouring rain, and as his vision improved, he could make out the figure of a man, hat pulled down low over his eyes, sitting just across from him. He appeared to be sleeping perhaps, or perhaps not...he didn't look the type to take a chance. A beat-up lever action rifle leaned against the sandstone wall beside him. The weapon had a telescopic sight, unusual in itself, but had obviously seen plenty of use over the years.

"How's the head?" the man asked quietly from under the hat's brim. He didn't appear to be a large man, hardly bigger than himself, Harley thought. There was a can with a familiar pork and beans label on it at his side, along with a thick bladed knife he'd used to open it.

Harley opened his other eye. "Any of those beans left?"

The man chuckled softly, as though to himself. "Not for you. I would have to untie you for that, and right now I'm just too tired. You should take off some weight, Harley Ponyboy, I had to drag you a long way here and it was not easy."

Harley turned his head a little and was rewarded with a stabbing pain at the back of his skull. "How is it you know my name?"

"Oh, I know a lot about you, Harley Ponyboy. When I was young, you would come to Eldon Bitsui's camp to herd sheep for him. I used to follow you around. It was said you were a tracker and knew this country better than anyone. I wanted to learn those things."

Harley tried to remember, despite the wracking pain in his head. "Are you his son? I didn't think Eldon had a son."

"He didn't have a son. Those old people never had any children. I was a pick-me-up like you."

"What about his daughter, Celia?"

"He didn't have a daughter either. Celia was a runaway. Eldon's wife took her in when she was in her teens and they raised her like their own. That is the kind of people they were, kind people. They should have had their own children, but for whatever reason, they didn't."

Harley flexed his shoulders, twisting slightly to see how tight the ropes might be. They were tight and well tied.

The man leaned forward, pushing back his hat, to smile at his captive. "You won't get out of those knots, Harley. That rawhide lariat got wet out there and I don't even know if I can get you out of them myself, without cutting them off. I would hate to do that; it took me a long time to braid that rope."

Harley nodded, sounding almost complacent when he said, "I don't guess it matters much does it? I expect you'll kill me now, anyway."

The man laughed outright at this. "I don't ever know who I'll kill, Harley, right up until the second I do it. There's some little thing in my head that tells me when. Like a little hair trigger in my brain. I guess I'm lucky that way, you know, being able to kill someone without thinking about it."

Taking a deep breath, Harley murmured, "I remember you now, John Etcitty. It was a long time ago, and that's not what you were called back then. I remember you as a skinny little boy named Frog. That was how Eldon Bitsui called you."

"Yes, and he still does call me that whenever I see him, which isn't often these days. I still try to go by there now and then...see if he needs anything, you know. But when Celia is there, I only watch from the ridge. She's never liked me, I don't know why. I've never done her any harm I can recall. For a long time I hoped she might get over it, but I guess she never did."

"She came to warn you last night, up there by the lightning tree." He paused a moment before saying, "Eldon sent her, I guess."

John Etcitty looked surprised at this, but tried to hide it with a frown, declaring, "I was there the day before. But you are right, I didn't come this morning."

Harley smiled past the dull aching pain pounding at his head. "Once I hit your trail, I could tell pretty quick the sign was at least a day old, but I figured they were your tracks, just the same."

"The woman said she'd seen you up there on the rim, when she brought the sheep down the other night."

Etcitty reached into a wooden box at the back of the shelter, bringing out a small tin pot which he set under a stream of water, still sluicing off the edge of the overhang. "Let's have us a little coffee Harley Ponyboy, to warm our bones." He placed a few small pieces of wood on the coals, then arranged them to quickly catch fire. Setting the pot of water to boil, he dumped in a handfull of ground coffee from a can before tipping the lid closed.

Harley saw the shelter had been used in the past and suspected the man might have several of these little hideouts spotted around the back country. He could tell Frog had lived this way a long time, alone for the most part, trusting in only a select few. By now he was a person attuned to his surroundings, and ever on his guard. It was no wonder he'd never been caught. If what Billy Red Clay said was true, he didn't even exist. Not officially anyway.

John Etcitty rubbed his hands together and beamed. "You are as good as you ever were Harley. I set you up several times this morning, but you shied off...outfoxed me both times."

"As good as I ever was, huh?" Harley attempted a grin. "That must be why I'm sitting here tied up and you're eating pork and beans."

"Well, there's that, but then again, you are not out here every day doing this. I am. That makes all the difference, I know that Harley. No, you are as good as you ever were. It just wasn't good enough this time." The man peered through a tiny plume of smoke, dropping one eyelid in a sly glance. "I hear you are a rich man now, Harley. Live in a fine house, with a son of your own, and a new Chevy truck to drive."

Harley shrugged, then after a moment asked. "So, are you the one who put a rattlesnake in my mailbox?"

"Rattlesnake!" Appearing to take offense, John Etcitty drew back. "I don't even know where you live, Harley. No, that wasn't me." he said chuckling. "That is not my style. What I would have done is lie in the weeds across from your house and shoot you when you came out in the morning. But the fact is, I haven't been to a town in years."

"Then I guess you weren't the one who took a shot at your Nephew, either?" Harley scowled. "He is just a boy for God's sakes. Don't try to tell me you didn't do that."

"Ah, yes, my Nephew. If I had meant to kill him, twice, do you think he would still be up and walking around? Not hardly. I would have hoped you'd give me more credit than that."

"But you might have killed him either of those times, by accident alone. That blow to the head could easily have been fatal."

The man waved this away. "I've hit many a man in the head, Harley. I know exactly what it takes to kill a person. Actually, I'm very good at it." He raised his two hands palms up. "Look at you my friend, you were knocked out a few hours, and yet here you are. As for that shot I took up above your camp, If I had meant to kill the boy, he would be dead. You can be sure of that."

Harley shook his head. "Why, would you do such things? It doesn't make sense. What did that boy do to you to bring you down on him like this? He is your sister's only child...your blood kin. Why?"

"That, Harley Ponyboy, is none of your business." Etcitty turned back to the fire and poured a large tin cup of coffee from the pot as he apologized, "I don't get many visitors up here, so we will have to share this cup. Give me a minute and I'll try to loosen your hands. It's not going to be easy, but we'll see what we can do." He stood up to stretch and swing his arms a time or two, then stepped around the fire pit to kneel down at Harley's side. "Oh my, this rawhide is drying faster than I thought. It's starting to shrink already." He made that 'tsk, tsk, tsk' sound which almost universally means something has gone awry. I'm afraid your hands are swelling—a little while longer and we might have had a problem here." Gingerly, he tried to untie the bindings, but in the end had to go back for his knife and then, almost gently, proceeded to sever each individual strand of braided rawhide. "I wish I didn't have to cut this Lariat up. It took me a long time to make it. But, still, I would hate to see you lose a hand over such a thing. You might not think it, Harley, but I'm not so cruel as some make me out to be. I've hurt people, yes, but I've never felt the need to be cruel along with it." The man stopped to examine the fingers on each of Harley's hands as he finished. "There, then," he said finally, peeling away the few remaining strands of lariat. "That should be better. Don't you think?"

Harley had lost all feeling in the hands, which were swollen and discolored. *It will take a while for the feeling to return.* He thought, *and when it does, it's going to hurt like Hell.* At least he hoped it would hurt, if it didn't, he might lose a couple of fingers - and that was the best-case scenario.

John Etcitty stared at the puffy, bluish colored flesh for some minutes, waiting as it were, for the circulation to return. Finally, losing patience, he said gruffly, "Rub your hands together, Harley. Rub them hard like this!" and he worked his two hands together in front of his face.

Harley tried his best, but without any feeling, he could only flop them together like mishappen mittens. He looked helplessly down at the hands, and shaking his head, muttered something under his breath then began slinging his wrists back and forth, thinking that might get the blood moving.

John Etcitty growling deep in his chest, grabbed first one and then the other of Harley's hands and rubbed them roughly between his own until he saw some slight change in color. "Ah, I think this is going to work, Harley, I believe these are going to get better now." He could see the hands were recovering somewhat and, with a grimace, said, "I would hate to think, I had crippled a good tracker like you, Harley." Moving back to the other side of the fire, he busied himself adding fresh wood to the coals and making more coffee. Sitting back, he appeared to contemplate this man he'd known as a young boy.

Harley continued rubbing his hands, frowning at the pain of renewed circulation. He gazed past the fire, wondering what Etcitty was thinking, and what had motivated him to do the things he had done. He seemed to be talking to himself now, and Harley looked away, but listened intently for some clue as to what he might have in mind.

John Etcitty had an odd look on his face as he stared into the flames, and could be heard to mutter, "I would rather see a man dead, than left crippled on my account."

Chapter 20

The Caldera

Charlie Yazzie considered himself a man of principal; one who stood behind those he considered close, no matter what. Now, two of his oldest friends, Harley Ponyboy and Thomas Begay, were stretching this precept to the limit. This time the two were testing his breaking point.

Navajo Policeman Billy Red Clay had called to say he was not only worried about the pair's safety but was also concerned they might be inadvertently alerting the very people he and Charlie were investigating. The lawmen's major focus had been to keep things low-key, and not push their suspects until iron clad charges could be filed. It was true Billy had gone out to Erwin Johnson's place, but that was only as a follow-up to the man's report of the, then missing Sam Klah. Johnson had surely expected someone might come, thinking it a natural consequence of his actions. Why the man would have reported the incident in the first place, if he meant the boy harm, was something neither lawman could figure out. Unless, of course, Johnson was fending off suspicions which might later be brought to bear. This was Billy's contention.

As far as Charlie was concerned, Erwin Johnson was already culpable in the phony investment scam, something he'd engineered long ago, and he could see no real connection to the man when it came to the attempts on Sam Klah's life. *What possible reason might Johnson have for harming the boy?*

Navajo Cop Billy Red Clay, on the other hand, could not be swayed, thinking Johnson could well have a part in the thing. Admittedly, this was only a gut feeling on his part. The Officer could offer no real evidence to support so boldfaced a supposition.

Charlie, preferring to fry one fish at a time, was concentrating his investigation on Erwin Johnson's investment scams. To that end, the Investigator was determined to bring him down using the charges he'd already documented. The death of Norman Klee had been a blow, but thanks to the old man he at least knew where to look, and what he was looking for. Attempted murder, without tangible proof was a hard row to hoe in his experience. Later in the afternoon, he would have reason to rethink this.

~~~~~~

The cold voice of Charlie Yazzie's receptionist came on the intercom, saying Human Services were on line three and needed to speak to him personally. Turning to the console, he picked up the phone and touched the blinking light. "Yazzie."

"Hey, Charlie...Bob Benally here...over at Human Services. We're told you might know the whereabouts of a young man named Sam Klah."

Charlie hesitated before asking, "And, what might this be about, Bob?"

"We've been trying to locate the boy in reference to a Government remediation settlement due his late mother, Lyla Klah." A rustle of papers was heard as the man verified the dates involved. "This is regarding an action filed some years ago, and only now adjudicated for payment. There was some question as to who the beneficiary of those funds should be. Our records show Sam Klah is underage at this point...not old enough to legally receive these funds. There would probably have to be the appointment of someone to look out for him until he's of age." The man paused before going on, "Usually, that would mean a close relative."

Charlie remained cautious. "As far as we know, the boy has only one blood relative, an Uncle we've, as yet been unable to contact. We're still working on that."

Bob didn't answer for a moment, with only a further rustling of papers in the interim. "That's odd. There's an old notation in Lyla Klah's file that indicating she may have had a half-brother as well, but no name is given."

Charlie mulled this over before answering, "Neither the FBI, nor anyone else, found any such thing."

"Well, let me take a further look. As I'm sure you know, people here on the reservation were prone to change names back then, sometimes without rhyme or reason as far as one can tell. I do know the man who put that note in Klah's file, he retired some years ago but still lives here. I'll talk to him and see if he remembers anything that might help. I'll get back to you on that, Charlie, then we can go from there."

Hanging up the phone, the Investigator swung his chair to the window overlooking the office. Most of the staff were out to lunch, leaving only a scattered few, mostly younger people, to contemplate their sack-lunches. As though in a daze, Charlie considered the possibility Sam Klah might have yet another Uncle. *Someone else in line to inherit his mother's hard-won reward for her many years suffering. And someone else with a motive for wanting the boy out of the way.*

Charlie's thoughts were interrupted by the sight of Billy Red Clay, coming through the front entrance, obviously in a hurry, but taking time to check in at the desk. The intercom light came on and, punching the button, Charlie said, "Send him on in, Arlene."

On his way back, Billy waved at someone he knew; a girl he'd gone to high school with and dated occasionally. Charlie smiled at this, and hoping it boded well for the cop's social life. The young man didn't get out enough in his opinion. *All work and no...*

Billy walked in without stopping to knock, as most of his friends were prone to do. At least Billy had bothered to check in. Not everyone did, not Thomas or Harley, for sure.

"Come on in Billy. Have you heard from your Uncle or Harley?"

"No, not a word. No one's seen or heard from them for two days now. I thought one of the patrolmen might have spotted them on one of their runs, but no one's seen hide nor hair of them.

Charlie grunted, "I'm not surprised. I've checked with everyone I can think of...nothing so far. Those two rascals know how to get lost when they want to."

Billy nodded and then, remembering what he came for, asked, "I guess you know Human Services is looking for Sam Klah?"

"They called. Was Bob who you talked to?"

"Yes. It seems he's having a hard time believing no one knows where the boy's gotten off to."

"What else did he have to say? I expect you were the first one he called?"

"Why would you say that?"

"Because you haven't mentioned the possibility Sam Klah has another Uncle."

"What the hell? You don't mean it?"

"It seems there was an old note in Lyla's file, suggesting she might have had two brothers. One being John Etcitty and the other, an unnamed half-brother." Charlie looked up from the notes he'd jotted down. "I must have jarred Bob's memory when I got excited about it, because he went back to the file and verified what the note alluded to. He says he'll check with someone who used to work there. It's his signature on the note and, though he's retired now, he may know something. Bob says he'll get back to me this afternoon...maybe."

Billy started to say something, but before he could get the words out of his mouth, Charlie held up a hand to stop him, and then smiled. "I know what you're thinking, Billy. Careful now you don't embarrass yourself.

We might know for sure soon enough, and then, maybe you can say, 'I told you so.'"

Billy laughed outright. "Charlie, this whole thing is weird. I wouldn't be surprised at anything now."

Billy was still smiling when the phone rang. The two men exchanged looks, as Charlie reached to pick up the handset.

"Yazzie." With a furrowed brow, Charlie held a finger up to Billy as he concentrated. "I see... yes, I understand. No, Billy's here now... I'll let him know." Several minutes passed as Charlie continued listening without speaking.

Hanging up, he pushed himself back from the desk as he raised his eyes to the ceiling. "Well, your hunch might be right, Billy. Bob says his source is a little shaky on some of the details, but he's certain about the alleged half-brother in the note. It seems there was such an outcry against the mining faction at the time, that Lyla Klah's legal action prompted him to add the note after talking to one of her relatives. Who, he claimed, was mentioned as a possible witness in her upcoming case. He recalled the person he interviewed used several names to refer to Lyla's half-brother, so he put a note in the file as a reminder to research it later. Of course, he never got back to it."

Charlie paused to catch his breath and Billy, unable to contain himself any longer, jumped in with both feet, exclaiming, "I know it's no 'smoking gun', but I'm getting that gut feeling again, Charlie."

The Investigator dead-panned this and held up a cautionary finger. "There's more, Billy, but before you get too excited, the relative that Human Services interviewer talked to, has been dead for nearly ten years." Shaking his head, he murmured, "Died of uranium poisoning himself."

Billy, somewhat deflated, sank back in his chair before asking, "But, there is more to the story...right?"

"There's more." Charlie conceded. "The old man did remember one of the names mentioned in that interview—because it was the same as his own brother's Navajo name. It stuck with him over the years just for that reason. The name was *Bidzill.*"

Billy was quick to pick up on this. "*Bidzill*? Hmm, that means, 'He is strong', or 'Strong Man' depending on how it's used."

Navajo Police Officers are required to be fluent in the language. This had been one of the big advantages Billy had when applying for the job. And again, later, when he was chosen Tribal Liaison Officer to the FBI. Charlie Yazzie, as a longtime supporter, had recommended him for both of those posts.

Charlie didn't consider himself as fluent in the Navajo tongue as Billy Red Clay, or even Thomas Begay, or Harley Ponyboy, for that matter. He had however, continued to expand his vocabulary over the years, and was satisfied he was fluent enough to do his job. When Charlie first returned home from the University, he was at a disadvantage among native speakers. Thomas Begay was quick to pick up on this, citing the new legal aid's need for a translator, he worked this to his advantage on several occasions.

One thing Charlie did know, was that *Bidzill* was not an uncommon name among older Navajo men, and thought, *everywhere we turn in this case there's a dead-end that brings us up short—we just can't catch a solid break.*

Chapter 21

The Problem

Harley Ponyboy had eaten his half-can of beans and finished the coffee as best he could before his hands were retied. Not so tight this time, but tight enough. His mind was clear now, allowing the reality of his predicament to sink in. His chance of escape, sadly, seemed impossible. John Etcitty meant to kill him, and that was the brutal fact of the matter. The man was toying with him.

Through half-closed eyes, Harley studied his tightly bound feet, totally immobilized. Though his stout work boots prevented any major loss of circulation, his feet were beginning to go numb. The stout, rawhide lariat, ran from his feet to his hands, then encircled his neck. Its end secured to a thick root behind him, and impossible to work free. John had, no doubt, done this before, and was well experienced at the work. Harley found himself immersed in recurring scenes of his capture. He cursed himself again and again for the stupidity that allowed this person to best him, in something he himself was so good at. He'd underestimated the man for a second time. There was only one hope now, and this became his focus as he pondered the bleak prospect of getting out of this alive.

Thomas Begay was out there. There was no doubt in his mind that he was holed up somewhere on his back-trail. He could only hope his friend found shelter as good as his during the storm. He was certain Thomas would have found his mule by now and that would mean he at least had food, such as it was.

Mule's feet are small, sinking deep in the mud to leave a good trail. There was the chance, despite the rain, Thomas had been able to track that mule back to where he'd been snatched off its back. Should this be the case, the man might be closer than he'd dared think. Two things were certain; his friend wouldn't give up, and he wouldn't give in. No matter the weather, or how hard the trail, Thomas Begay would, sooner or later, find him. He smiled grimly into the dark of night, hoping against hope his friend would come while he was still alive. Either way, Thomas would be here by and by, and then there would be hell to pay. He had to believe that. All he had to do now, was stay alive.

It was near midnight as far as Harley could figure, and the heavy rain that pounded them earlier in evening had tapered off to a misty drizzle. The fresh smell of pinion pine wafting through the shelter refreshed his senses, buoying his spirit. Gazing across the smoldering embers at Etcitty, Harley thought to himself, *I don't remember Frog being very smart as a boy... But then, neither was I. Outwitting him might be a close one.*

John Etcitty, lolling on one elbow, and only occasionally looking up to check on his miserable captive, was first to speak, "How was the coffee and beans, my friend? I hope they filled you up, 'cause that's all we got right now. I try to keep a little something in all my hidey holes, but we already went through that. I hadn't really planned on company. Still, I'm glad I had a little something for you, at least. I'll bet you had food in your saddle bags. I went looking for your mule you know, while you were knocked out. Having that mule, would have been a lot handier than dragging you all the way up here." He slapped his knee as he laughed, "But, Harley, that Damned mule took off like a shot. Acted like he was going to run clear out of the country—probably what he had in mind, too. But I'll bet he's back down there at old man Eldon's place now. Don't you think so? Mules don't like to be by themselves much, do they?" John was silent a moment, contemplating each word before going on. "I guess nobody likes to be alone. Except me." He smiled at this, then sighing heavily, canted his head a little to stare at Harley. "My Brother tells me you're a rich man now, is that true? Are you rich, Harley?" Raising himself to a sitting position, Etcitty pursed his lips in a thin smile, and said, "I know I'm running off at the mouth here, Harley, but I don't often get a chance to talk to anyone—and for sure not someone I used to look up to. I never looked up to many. I can tell you that."

Harley, surprised at this, called to him in Navajo, as he might have as a boy. "*Ch'al*," he said, using the Navajo word for Frog. "I don't remember you having a brother, but it's been a long time, I might have forgotten. This brother of yours, he told you I was rich? No. I'm not really rich, not like some people, I have a little money now, yes, but it's not as much you'd think. You tell your brother that, next time you see him."

Chuckling, Etcitty was quick to set Harley straight. "He's only my half-brother. He had a different father and a different name, but you know how our people are. They think if two men have the same mother, then they are as much brothers as it gets. But, you know, Harley, I never liked him and he never liked me. He's the reason I used to come up here to Eldon Bitsui's place whenever I could and herd sheep for him. I couldn't have been more than twelve or thirteen years old at the time. My mother was always holding this brother up to me, telling me how he was going to make something of himself someday. She always said, 'Strong Man will be somebody.' Frog turned away to hide his face for a moment, and then looked down at the fire.

Harley could see the glowing coals reflected in his eyes and was certain that he saw the devil in them.

"You asked me before why I tried to kill my own nephew, someone I didn't even know. Well, I'm going to tell you why, since one or the other of us is going to be dead before this is all over. So, it really doesn't matter if you know, or not." He settled himself back against the wall and began to talk in a low voice, surreal in the cave-like shelter. "Sometime back, my so-called brother came to see me. He'd always known where to get in touch with me. He understood my ties to Eldon Bitsui, but this was the first time he dared come out here to talk to me face to face. He knew my reputation, and how I felt about him, but still he came, saying he had a business proposition for me. One that could make me a lot of money. He went on to say he would pay me to locate my nephew and do away with him, and then, when our sister's settlement finally came through, he would split it with me half and half." He paused to smile at this, before going on.

"It was then that I decided to go along with him for a while, just to see if he had changed in any way. Not that it mattered really, but at the time it seemed important. The money meant nothing to me. Look around you Harley, this is how I live. Money won't make it better. I chose this path a long time ago. Someday someone, like you maybe, will run across me at just the right moment, and it will all be over. It's just as simple as that, Harley. I'm living on borrowed time."

"What about your nephew? That boy doesn't mean anything to you?"

"Not really, I never knew him. I'm like my brother in that way, I guess. Neither of us has room in our hearts for anyone but ourselves. When it came right down to it, I could have killed that boy, you know, either of those two times, but that would have ended the game. I was beginning to enjoy that part of it...just as I'm enjoying our short time together now, Harley." John Etcitty grew silent, making way for a brooding sadness falling over him like a dark cloak. Mumbling incoherently, he was, once again, alone with himself.

Dawn was not far off, a few small birds could be heard twittering in the trees nearby. A distant coyote yelped its way into a thin howl, calling its nearly grown pups. The sound faded as the nocturnal breeze changed direction in the grey of another morning.

Harley Ponyboy wondered if Thomas was up and, on his way, or...if he'd lost the trail and would not make it in time. John Etcitty would want to be on the move soon and he wouldn't be dragging anyone along with him. He had no more than thought this when he suddenly realized the birds had fallen silent. He peered across at John Etcitty, to see if he too had noticed, but the man was stirring the coals, possibly thinking he might have enough coffee to make a final cup. Those birds might have gone quiet for any number of reasons; a fox slinking through, or an owl, maybe, ghosting from pine to pine. Maybe John *had* noticed, but he'd given no sign, if he had.

Harley tried to set up a little straighter, twisting and turning to draw his captor's attention.

As the embers flared, Etcitty stood suddenly and without word or expression, picked up his rifle, and moved cautiously to the front of the shelter, peering into the darkness. "Almost morning, Harley," he called quietly, "I refilled the pot before it quit raining last night. Maybe we can have a last cup together."

Harley followed the man with his eyes to see him suddenly tense, clutch his rifle tighter, then jerk backward as the thunder of a shot reverberated through the shelter. Sagging slightly, he turned to him before crumpling to his knees only feet away.

"You see how it is, Harley…" His rasping breath came in gulps as he fixed the bound man with a look of calm disbelief. A froth of red bubbled from his lips and he coughed, struggling for air. The shadow of a smile appeared and he managed to say, "You won't have to notify my brother." He shuddered as he mumbled his final words. "I already notified *Bidzill*."

At the sound of another cartridge being levered in Harley tore his eyes from the dying man, looking up to see Thomas Begay, soaking wet, saddle gun leveled for another shot. The words caught in his throat. "Don't shoot him no more, Thomas. He's done."

Thomas lowered the rifle slightly and watched as the fatally wounded man pushed his hands out before him and then with a groan, John Etcitty laid himself down for the last time.

Chapter 22

The Calling

It was early afternoon when Charlie Yazzie and Officer Red Clay arrived at the Johnson place. Charlie still thought the trip was a long shot, but Billy was convinced Erwin might help them locate Thomas and Harley, and eventually had talked the Investigator into it.

Billy parked the Tribal unit close in, with a good view of the house, and the two lawmen spent a few moments looking the place over. Seeing no vehicle, and no one in sight, the Cop nudged his friend and gave a push of his chin toward the front door...plainly standing ajar. "No dog around either," he whispered.

The men stepped down from the truck as Billy unsnapped the tiedown on his service revolver. The two moved silently onto the porch and with another quick look around, Billy cautiously pushed the door open. The smell alone was warning enough to let them know something was bad wrong. They glanced at one another and Billy took the lead, warily stepping inside, only to pull up short. Gagging, he pulled out a bandana and covered his nose. Charlie quickly followed suit as they eased into the front room. They spotted the body at the same time—just through the door to the kitchen—sprawled across the linoleum floor in that macabre posture common to people whose death came as a surprise. Blood seeped from under the corpse to form a dry black ring. Billy nodded toward the remains, murmuring through the cloth, "That's Erwin Johnson."

Charlie considered this for a moment. "The Bureau will want us to back out of this one, Billy. We'd best leave things as they are. That's the law. The FBI's investigation takes precedence."

Billy concurred, with a nod, and after one final look, the pair retraced their steps to the front porch.

Charlie spoke first. "Looked to me like a knife was what killed him."

As a traditional thinking *Diné*, Billy Red Clay had a problem being near the dead and was forced to steel himself each time the job required it. His face took on an unnatural shade of gray—his hand shaking as he took hold of a post to steady himself. Lifting his nose to the breeze, he sucked in a long draught of cold air before speaking, "Erwin had a good dog here last time I came, but I don't see him now. I don't see his truck either. You don't suppose whoever did this, took it...and maybe the dog, too?" He shook his head at the observation. "It wasn't the sort of dog to run off." He continued surveying the property with a skeptical eye.

"Well, that's a real possibility I guess." Charlie looked up the road they'd come in on. "How far to the nearest place you can radio in? Fred will want to get some people out here, the quicker the better, considering how far along the body is."

Billy thought a moment. "It's seven or eight miles to Standing Hill. I've had good reception from up there before, when the weather is right." The Policeman thought for a moment. "There's a radiotelephone at the Trader's too, but that's a good bit farther."

Charlie nodded. "We better head that direction. We can try the Hill first, but if not that, it will have to be the trading post."

"So, where does this leave us, Charlie?"

"Well, Officer Red Clay, I would think, once again, we are at a proverbial dead end. At least in the case of Erwin Johnson's fraud charges. Not only does his death bring that investigation to an end, but most likely, the death of Norman Klee. The exact cause of *his* death may forever remain a mystery. That's the way it looks to me, at least right now it does."

Billy sighed and silently nodded. "When we know who killed Erwin Johnson, we might have the key to the whole business. That's what I think."

Charlie gave the young Policeman a wan smile. "We still have an ace in the hole, such as it is. It will be interesting to see what your Uncle and Harley Ponyboy might have turned up. Harley knows the country, and he knows the right people. At some point, there's a good chance someone will talk to Harley." Then swinging an arm toward the horizon, he said, "Doubtless, those boys have been busy the last couple of days. They might well have heard something, sitting in a warm *hogan* somewhere, sipping hot coffee with a local." Smiling at the thought, he went on. "In any case, I know those rascals well enough to say they've been turning over some rocks. We'll hear from them eventually, I expect."

~~~~~~

When Billy Red Clay pulled into Charlie's drive, the first thing they noticed was Harley's pickup parked beside his house, still loaded with gear. His horse trailer sat by the corrals, and Charlie satisfied himself that the mules standing at the fence included the bulk of the herd.

Billy Red Clay was grinning as he dropped the Investigator off at his house at the end of the lane. "I'm sure we'll be hearing some wild stories from these two in the next day or so. No matter what might actually have happened."

Waving each other goodbye, the two parted company content in the knowledge the troublemakers were at last in hand.

Sue had waited up for him, and no doubt with his dinner waiting in the oven. As he'd expected, she was in the kitchen—Little Harley sitting beside her in his highchair drinking milk. The boy looked up and waved a spoon. Charlie went to sit by him as Sue retrieved his dinner and brought it to the table.

"He won't go to bed again, huh?"

"Not yet, he said he wanted to wait up for you."

"His father didn't take him when he got home?"

"It's a long story. Harley did come by for him but was so worn out he could barely keep his eyes open, let alone take care of the baby. I told him to go home and get some sleep. I can't imagine how the man was able to drive home and unload those mules." She hesitated slightly before going on. "He and I talked for a few minutes, though." Throwing a glance at the baby, she put a finger to her lips.

"I'll tell you what he had to say, later."

Charlie turned to the boy, grinning at the shock of black hair sticking straight up in a bush. The boy regarded him from eyes black as coal as he grinned back. "Hi," the little fellow said, turning back to his cup of milk.

Charlie shook his head. "I swear, this boy looks more like Harley every day."

"I *am* Harley," the three-year-old declared confidently.

Charlie chuckled. "Yes, you are. You are for a fact Harley Ponyboy."

Only a few minutes later the boy began to nod. The next thing they knew his eyes were closed and he was fast asleep. Sue smiled at her husband as he lifted the boy out of the chair and carried him to his bed.

Returning to the kitchen, Charlie sighed heavily as he sat himself down. "Out like a light... So, where did Harley say they've been? What happened up there?"

Sue touched her chin in thought. "All he said was, they ran into a little trouble up north, but that Sam Klah was safe now." She turned to listen a moment as the wind rattled the kitchen windows. "Thomas Begay is in jail."

~~~~~

Thomas slouched against the passenger side door with only the occasional glance at Charlie Yazzie, keeping his own council. The Investigator stared straight ahead as he drove. Possibly thinking he could wait him out. Something he'd seldom been able to do.

The Lanky Navajo hadn't said a word since he got in the truck and both men were prepared for an uncomfortable drive back home. By the time they crossed the La Plata bridge, however, Thomas began to talk, and didn't stop until he'd told his old friend the entire story.

Before picking him up, Charlie had skimmed through the official report, but he listened intently to Thomas's version of the narrative before commenting. "What did Fred say when you told him what happened?"

"He said, it sounded like self-defense. We were both armed and Etcitty was already raising his rifle when I shot. Harley saw the whole thing and backed me all the way."

"I'm sure he did."

"Harley also told Fred, that just before Etcitty died, he pretty much confessed to killing his half-brother."

"What do you mean, 'He pretty much confessed?'"

He was talking Navajo, so Harley had a good idea what he meant from the way he phrased it.

Charlie looked thoughtfully out the window. "I talked to Fred first thing this morning, he said there would be an inquest, but didn't think it would amount to much. He also spoke to the Judge who agreed to release you into my custody until the hearing. Senior Agent Fred Smith is all right in my book. He thinks you saved the Bureau a lot of trouble."

Thomas smiled for the first time. "Just like old times...huh, Charlie?"

Charlie coughed, and with a frown, grudgingly nodded his head. "I guess so... I was hoping you would eventually grow out of this sort of thing but..." The Investigator was still frowning when he said. "As it turns out, Agents found Erwin's truck parked at the trailhead, his dog was roaming around up there, too. It must have gotten loose from Etcitty." Charlie had a last thought. "Oh, yeah, the knife that killed Johnson... It was recovered from the truck, as well."

With a grim set to his jaw, Thomas turned to the Investigator and declared. "Harley Ponyboy's life was on the line up there you know, I did what I had to do, and I don't regret it."

"I know you didn't have much choice Thomas. I'd hoped it would end another way, but like you said, you did what you had to do."

Thomas nodded, satisfied his old friend understood. Turning back to the window, he spoke again, but softer this time. "One thing's for sure. The people up in that country will sleep better now that John Etcitty is gone. And Sam Klah won't have to be looking over his shoulder anymore either."

"Speaking of Sam Klah, you may as well know, he's coming into a lot of money soon. What do you think Ida Marie will have to say about that?"

"Why, she'll think it's wonderful her father's giving them his blessing." Thomas chuckled along with Charlie but was serious when he said. "I did hear an interesting little story in jail, just drunks talking of course, but it gave me a pretty good idea who put that rattler in Harley's mailbox."

Charlie looked up, surprised. "Who was it, for God's sake?"

"Just an old drunk me and Harley had a little tussle with. It was a long time ago. He was probably jealous Harley has done so well and that was his way of getting back at him. The man's mind is about gone, and by the time he gets out of jail, this time, it won't matter anyway." He gave Charlie a pointed look. "I don't think we should say anything about any of this to Harley, no need in getting him started again. You know how he is."

Charlie wondered at this a moment, saying, "I just hope he can put all this behind him now."

Thomas turned to face him. "Oh, I think he may already have. He met a woman up there on the *Tse' Bii' Ndzigaii*. He tells me he's going back next week and taking little Harley with him. He wants the boy to meet old Eldon Bitsui and his daughter. He wants to see if Celia and his son take to one another. She is a fine-looking woman and with a temperament suited for raising a child. Of course, I don't know that anything will come of any of this. Harley is still Harley." He thought a moment longer. "I personally, don't see how he could do any better."

Charlie, shaking his head, smiled. "Well good for him, Little Harley can be a handful at times. I expect he could use a little help raising him."

The two Navajo rode homeward in silence, each in his own mind confident the stars were aligning as they should and thinking brighter days might lie ahead for them all.

Such is the way of man. Regardless of origin or race or color, the eternal flame burns brightest in those who have known darkness.

R. Allen Chappell

Addendum

These stories hearken back to a slightly more traditional time on the reservation, and while the places and culture are real, the characters and their names are fictitious. Any resemblance to actual persons living or dead is purely coincidental.

~~~~~~

Though this book is a work of fiction, a concerted effort was made to maintain the accuracy of the culture and life on the reservation. There are many scholarly tomes written by anthropologists, ethnologists, and learned laymen regarding Navajo culture. On the subject of language and spelling, they often do not agree. When no consensus was apparent, we have relied upon 'local knowledge.'

Many changes have come to the *Dinè*—some of them good—some, not so much. These are the Navajo I remember. I think you may like them.

ABOUT THE AUTHOR

R. Allen Chappell is the author of eleven novels and a collection of short stories. Growing up in New Mexico he spent a good portion of his life at the edge of the *Diné Bikeyah*, went to school with the Navajo, and later worked alongside them. He now lives in Western Colorado where he continues to pursue a lifelong interest in the prehistory of the Four Corners region and its people, past and present. He still spends a good bit of his time there.

For the curious, the author's random thoughts on each book of the series are listed below in the order of their release.

Navajo Autumn

It was not my original intent to write a series, but this first book was so well received, and with many readers asking for another, I felt compelled to write a sequel—after that there was no turning back. And while I have to admit this first one was fun to write, I'm sure I made every mistake a writer can possibly make in a first novel. I did, however, have the advantage of a dedicated little group of detractors, quick to point out its deficiencies... and I thank them. Without that help, this first book would doubtless have languished, and eventually fallen into the morass.

Navajo Autumn was the first in its genre to include a glossary of Navajo words and terms. Readers liked this feature so well I've made certain each subsequent book had one. This book has, over the years, been through many editions and updates. No book is perfect, and this one keeps me grounded.

Boy Made of Dawn

A sequel I very much enjoyed writing and one that drew many new fans to the series. So many, in fact, I quit my day job to pursue writing these stories full-time—not a course I would ordinarily recommend to an author new to the process. In this instance, however, it proved to be the right move. As I learn, I endeavor to make each new book a little better and try to keep their prices low enough that people like me can afford to read them. That's important.

Ancient Blood

The third book in the series and the initial flight into the realm of the Southwestern archaeology I grew up with. This book introduces Harley Ponyboy, a character that quickly carved out a major niche for himself in the stories that followed. Harley remains the favorite of reservation readers to this day. Also debuting in this novel was Professor George Armstrong Custer, noted archaeologist and Charlie Yazzie's professor at UNM. George, too, has a pivotal role in some of the later books.

Mojado

This book was a departure in subject matter, cover art, and the move to thriller status. A fictional story built around a local tale heard in Mexico years ago. In the first three months following its release, this book sold more copies, than any of the previous books. It's still a favorite.

Magpie Speaks

A mystery/thriller that goes back to the beginning of the series and exposes the past of several major characters—some of whom play key roles in later book—and are favorites of Navajo friends who follow these stories.

Wolves of Winter

As our readership attained a solid position in the genre, I determined to tell the story I had, for many years, envisioned. I am pleased with this book's success on several levels, and in very different genres. I hope one day to revisit this story in one form or another.

The Bible Seller

Yet another cultural departure for the series; Harley Ponyboy again wrests away the starring role. A story of attraction and deceit against a backdrop of wanton murder and reservation intrigue—it has fulfilled its promise to become a Canyon land's favorite.

Day of the Dead

Book eight in the series, and promised follow-up to #1 bestseller, Mojado. Luca Tarango's wife returns to take Luca's remains back to Mexico and inveigles Legal Services Investigator Charlie Yazzie to see that she and Luca's ashes get there for the Mexican holy day.

The Collector

Book number Nine in the series brings most of the original characters into play, but centers around Lucy Tallwoman. The murder of her agent causes her life to spiral out of control as unseen forces seek to take over the lucrative Native Arts trade. Danger and excitement abound in a book I very much enjoyed writing.

Falling Girl

Book ten—Again, reservation favorite Harley Ponyboy steals this one with his rags to riches tale of lost love, deceit, and newfound happiness. A reservation adventure to warm the coldest heart.

R. Allen Chappell

From the Author

Readers may be pleased to know they can preview selected audio book selections for the Navajo Nation Series on our book pages. Our Audio books can be found featured in public libraries, on Audible, and Tantor Audio Books and, of course, in many retail outlets. There are more to come. Kaipo Schwab, an accomplished actor and storyteller, narrates the first five audio books. I am delighted Kaipo felt these books worthy of his considerable talent. My hope is that you'll like these reservation adventures as much as we enjoy bringing them to you.

The author calls Western Colorado home where he continues to pursue a lifelong interest in the prehistory of the Four Corners region and its people. We remain available to answer questions, and welcome your comments at: rachappell@yahoo.com

If you've enjoyed this latest story, please consider going to its Amazon book page to leave a short review. It takes only a moment and would be most appreciated.

Glossary

1. *Adáánii* — undesirable, alcoholic etc.
2. *Acheii* — Grandfather *
3. *Ashki Ana'dlohi* — Laughing boy
4. *A-hah-la'nih* — affectionate greeting*
5. *Billigaana* — white people
6. *Bidzill* — Strong Man, or He is strong
7. *Ch'al* — Frog
8. *Ch'ihónit't* — a spirit path flaw in art
9. *Chindi* — (or *chinde*) Spirit of the dead *
10. *Diné* — Navajo people
11. *Diné Bikeyah* — Navajo country
12. *Diyin dine'é* — Holy people
13. *Dibe* — Sheep
14. *Hataalii* — Shaman (Singer)*
15. *Hastiin* — (Hosteen) Man or Mr. *
16. *Hogan* — (Hoogahn) dwelling or house
17. *Hozo* — To walk in beauty *
18. *Ma'ii* — Coyote
19. *Shimásáni* — Grandmother
20. *Shimá* — Mother
21. *Shizhé'é* — Father *
22. *Telii* — *Burro, or Donkey*
23. *Tsé Bii' Ndzisgaii* — Monument Valley
24. *Yaa' eh t'eeh* — Common greeting—Hello
25. *Yeenaaldiooshii* — Skinwalker, witch*
26. *Yóó'a'hááskahh* — One who is lost

*See Notes on following page

Notes

1. *Acheii* — Grandfather. There are several words for Grandfather depending on how formal the intent and the gender of the speaker.

2. *Aa'a'ii* — Long known as a trickster or "thief of little things." It is thought Magpie can speak and sometimes brings messages from the beyond.

4. *A-hah-la'nih* — A greeting: affectionate version of *Yaa' eh t'eeh*, generally only used among family and close friends.

9. *Chindi* — When a person dies inside a *hogan*, it is said that his *chindi* or spirit could remain there forever, causing the *hogan* to be abandoned. *Chindi* are not considered benevolent entities. For the traditional Navajo, just speaking a dead person's name may call up his *chindi* and cause harm to the speaker or others.

14. *Hataalii* — Generally known as a "Singer" among the *Diné*, they are considered "Holy Men" and have apprenticed to older practitioners sometimes for many years—to learn the ceremonies. They make the sand paintings that are an integral part of the healing and know the many songs that must be sung in the correct order.

15. *Hastiin* — The literal translation is "man" but is often considered the word for "Mr." as well. "Hosteen" is the usual version Anglos use.

17. *Hozo* — For the Navajo, "*hozo*" (sometimes *hozoji*) is a general state of well-being, both physical and spiritual, that indicates a certain "state of grace," which is referred to as "walking in beauty." Illness or depression is the usual cause of "loss of *hozo*," which may put one out of sync with the people as a whole. There are ceremonies to restore *hozo* and return the ailing person to a oneness with the people.

15. *Ma'ii* — The Coyote is yet another reference to one of several Navajo tricksters. The word is sometimes used in a derogatory sense or as a curse word.

21. *Shizhé'é* — (or *Shih-chai*) There are several words for "Father," depending on the degree of formality intended and sometimes even the gender of the speaker.

25. *Yeenaaldiooshii* — These witches, as they are often referred to, are the chief source of evil or fear in traditional Navajo superstitions. They are thought to be capable of many unnatural acts, such as flying or turning themselves into werewolves and other ethereal creatures; hence the term Skinwalkers, referring to their ability to change forms or skins.

Printed in Great Britain
by Amazon